BY

MATT HARRY

CODEX ARCANUM PRESS

Published by Codex Arcanum, Inc., Los Angeles, California
www.codexarcanumpress.com

Edited by Kaitlin Severini
Cover design and illustrations by Juliane Crump
Interior layout by Polgarus Studio

ISBN: 9781736502600
e-ISBN: 9781736502617
First edition

Printed in the United States of America

For Ronan & Milo, super in every way

What makes somebody a superhero?

Is it extraordinary powers? A desire to do good? Spandex?

Beats me. I'm just a regular thirteen-year-old who got caught up in a huge conspiracy involving drug dealers, meteorites, the Department of Homeland Security, and some really mean Internet trolls.

And technically, my baby sister's the one with the powers. Say hi, Val.

Heh-do.

She's cute, right? Basically I'm, like, her handler. Or her trainer. Whatever you wanna call it, I am definitely *not* her sidekick. Got it? Yeah, she might have been the one on the cover of *Time* magazine, but if it weren't for me, no one would even know she exists. And yes, I suppose you could argue that I'm *also* the reason we're sitting on the Golden Gate Bridge right now, one hundred and fifty feet off the ground, with a bunch of gun-toting mercenaries looking to use us as target practice. Sorry, Brynn and Dad. I never thought this would get so out of—

You know what? Let me start over.

Take two.

My name is Robbie Rampino, and this is my confession. For those of you who have been living in a bomb shelter for the last year, we're Superkid. Well, actually, my little sister is Superkid, and I'm . . . the kid who made her famous. There's been a lot of crap said about both of us in the last few months, so I'm here to set the record straight. Tell the world how all this really came to be.

Also, I'm pretty sure we're about to die.

So here it is—the true story of Superkid.

I stopped recording on the iPhone strapped to my wrist and looked out over the blinking lights of San Francisco. It was cool for August. Bracing. The wind was strong up here, whipping through the bay like it couldn't wait to get to Ghirardelli Square and buy some sourdough. Sure, the view was pretty, but it didn't give me any ideas about what to say next. Where should I begin? How does someone explain the origins of the world's first infant superhero? What would Stan Lee do?

"Ba-ba?" said Val. My sister was almost a year old, and annoyingly adorable. She was strapped to my chest in a black baby carrier. Her head was protected by a tiny, padded helmet with a purple SK logo stuck to the front. Chin-length black hair framed a heart-shaped face the color of an oatmeal cookie. Large hazel eyes blinked behind her helmet visor, crinkling the beauty mark next to her right eye. Her lower lip pooched out in a pouty frown, a clear tell she was about to start fussing.

"Seriously?" I whispered. "You know we're in mortal danger, right?"

"Ba-ba, ba-ba," said Val, opening and closing her fist in the sign for *milk*. Now her lower lip began to quiver. *Crap.* I had maybe two minutes, tops, until she had a full-on food fit.

"Okay, okay," I said quickly. I felt along the length of my utility belt. Next to the small baby wipe dispenser was a bandolier that held up to three eight-ounce bottles of formula. Thank the Maker, there was one left.

I shook the bottle, peering over the edge of the small maintenance platform on which I was crouched. The red metal cables of the Golden Gate Bridge were about three feet across, but the platform was only forty-eight inches. Not exactly built for lounging.

One hundred and fifty feet beneath us, three roided-out thugs in ski masks and body armor prowled the pedestrian bridge. A white, flaming bird was sewn into their masks. Their semiautomatic handheld Uzis were, for the moment, concealed. One thug, thinking outside the box, was scanning the bridge cable, but for the moment, he was focused on the wrong one.

"Here we go, Valley. Ba-ba's coming." I unscrewed the cap from Val's milk bottle. Removed a plastic nipple from the small zippered pouch on my belt. Placed it on top of the bottle . . . just as a gust of wind body-slammed into me.

I skidded several inches across the slick maintenance platform. My left hand instinctively grabbed for the guyline, and Val's bottle slipped from my hand. I watched helplessly as it spiraled through the air, spraying formula before hitting the concrete far below.

My sister saw it fall too, and she knew what it meant.

No ba-ba.

Her lips parted, and a piercing, hangry wail echoed over San Francisco Bay. I know most babies are loud, but Val's screams were special. A lumber mill sawing a thousand jackhammers in half couldn't drown her out. So it was no surprise that, when I peeked over the edge of the maintenance platform, I saw three ski mask–covered faces staring directly at our hiding spot.

What did surprise me was the speed of their response. They ran straight for the thin metal suspension wires that hung down from the red cable on which I was sitting, and they began to climb. Hand over hand, with the speed of military-trained, genetically enhanced killer apes.

"Okay, Valley. It's okay," I lied. As I patted her back, I weighed my options. If I went back down, they'd simply take out their Uzis and shoot me. If I went farther up the bridge cable, they'd climb after me and shoot me. Option B had the possibility of extending my life by a few more seconds, so I got to my feet. The cable curved up and away from me, leading to the top of the iconic red bridge tower like a level in *Sonic the Hedgehog*.

I shook my hands to warm up my cold fingertips, then fished Val's pacifier out of my belt pouch. "Here you go," I said, pressing the rubber plug to her lips. "Want a little binky to distract you? Binky-winky? No pressure or anything."

She complained, but took the rubber plug into her mouth and began to suck vigorously. The pacifier would buy me another five minutes or so, but if I didn't get something in her belly soon, the three murderers chasing us would be the least of my problems.

Wrapping my fingerless gloves securely around the guylines to either side of the cable, I began to jog upward. Val bounced against my chest. Sweat immediately collected in the more padded areas of my black leather duster. The visor of my motorcycle helmet began to fog up. I could have taken it off, but preserving our identities was currently more important than seeing or comfort.

I felt like a termite scrabbling up a huge, wet spaghetti noodle. My thigh muscles began to burn after the first few feet. My breath came in short, whistling gasps. The baby strapped to my chest felt like she weighed more than my granddad's Buick.

There was a *thump* behind me. A vibration thrummed through the cable under my feet. I turned, seeing our first pursuer had finished his climb. There was now only fifty feet of Golden Gate cable between us.

He had at least a hundred pounds on me, all of it rock-hard, battle-trained muscle. Yellow teeth gleamed in the mouth of his ski mask. His pupils were huge and jittery. That's not me being colorful—the dude's eyes were actually vibrating in their sockets. He was on Fortis for sure. I could have hit him with a wrecking ball, and he would have shrugged it off. He rolled his neck, making the vertebrae pop like Bubble Wrap. Then he began to sprint toward me.

I tried to pick up the pace, but by the time I reached the next maintenance platform, Yellow Teeth had nearly caught up to me. I was going to have to fight him.

I clambered on top of the platform. My fingers fumbled at my utility belt. Sweat ran into my eyes, stinging of salt and fear. I pulled out a small plastic bottle, twisted the cap, and pointed it at the face of my pursuer. When his fingers were two inches from my face, I squeezed.

Poof. A cloud of baby powder hit Yellow Teeth right in his ski mask–covered face. He coughed, swatting at his eyes. His thick-soled combat boots backpedaled on the slippery cable. He might have trained his body to absorb hot metal shrapnel in a war zone, but baby powder? That was clearly a new experience. His face twisted in uncontrollable agony, and he sneezed.

The force of it was enough to send him tumbling off the cable. His body fell past the suicide net beside the bridge and he continued dropping, five hundred feet straight down. He hit the cold, choppy waters of San Francisco Bay, never making a sound. Had it been me, I would have screamed the whole way down.

I watched the water for a long moment, holding my breath—and then Yellow Teeth splashed to the surface. Relief flooded through me. His legs were sure to be shattered from the fall, but thanks to the Fortis, he wouldn't feel that for a while. The important thing was, I hadn't committed my first murder.

Yellow Teeth's buddies paused in their climb up the suspension cables, looking down at their fallen comrade. Then, in the manner of well-trained Dobermans, their heads swiveled back toward me. Their black eyes vibrated like marbles in an earthquake. They continued to climb.

Within moments, the next mercenary reached my cable and pulled himself up, making sure to keep one hand on a guyline. As he jogged toward me, I reviewed my fighting options. The baby powder trick wouldn't work a second time. I scrolled through a mental list of my inventory—baby wipes, pureed food pouches, a squeezy giraffe—nothing that could fend off a drugged-up mercenary. But there was something in my backpack that might help.

I crouched behind the metal platform, my legs quivering in exhaustion. As I pulled off my backpack, Val spat out her binky. I caught it with the practiced hand of someone who's played this game a million times, and nudged it back in her mouth.

"Hang in there," I whispered, not sure if I was talking to her or myself. I rummaged through the backpack, pushing aside spare diapers, chewed-up board books, and the occasional stray Cheerio until I found what I'd been searching for.

Diaper cream. I flicked open the cap with my thumb, pointed it at the cable in front of me, and squeezed. The white slimy substance splatted on the red metal just in front of the approaching mercenary. His boots drew near my trap—and then he simply hopped over it. Stupid SEAL team reflexes. He landed on the metal platform in front of me, his fingers stretching for me like five sturdy fishhooks.

I let out a high-pitched squeal, backpedaled up the cable, slipped, and landed solidly on my butt. Real Bruce Lee stuff. The impact popped the binky out of Val's mouth, and she immediately wailed in annoyance. I kept crab-walking, my mind an idea-free whiteboard of panic.

Val's crying increased in volume. "Stay back," I said to the mercenary. "Don't make me use her powers on you."

The thug chuckled. "Hand over the bambino," he said in a Southern drawl, "and I won't chuck your scrawny middle-school butt offa this here bridge."

"No offense," I said, "but you don't exactly seem like the 'responsible caregiver' type. You know how to change a diaper? Perform infant CPR? I at least need to see some references."

"Quit stallin'," the Kentucky Fried thug said. "I might be gettin' paid for this gig, but it ain't so much that I won't shoot you for annoying me."

Before I could craft another witty response, the mercenary lunged at me.

Now, before I describe what happened next, let me first state that I'm aware of what a horrible, irresponsible brother I was. I knew that many people referred to Val's crime-fighting career as "child abuse." And I knew that if I'd been a different kind of sibling, we wouldn't be running from mercenaries five hundred feet above shark-infested waters. We probably never would have become superheroes in the first place. Val could have lived her entire life in safety, without anyone else knowing what she could do.

But no matter what you might think, I've always tried to keep my sister safe. Keep that in mind before you rush to judge me, okay? Because what I did next, I did to save the both of us.

I jumped off the Golden Gate Bridge.

For one, heart-stopping second, the only thing between me and the earth's crust was a whole lot of salty San Francisco air. Then my hands closed around the guyline. Gravity pulled my skeleton downward like a Slinky. The thin metal twanged, but for the moment, it held. I looked back up at the cable. Kentucky Fried Thug gave me a crooked grin.

"Gutsy move, boy," he said, taking out his Uzi. "But how you gonna dodge this?"

Brrrrap! A burst of gunfire sparked off the guyline less than five feet away from me. The thin metal snapped and frayed, but for the moment, it held.

"Swing on back now," KFT said, "or the next burst goes in your leg."

"No thanks," I said. Not the best comeback, but most of my brain was occupied with thoughts of my imminent death. The frayed wire popped again—

And then it snapped. The mercenary's eyes widened. He knelt down to grab me, but Val and I were long gone, swinging toward the bridge tower like two Tarzans on a slick metal vine. That might look fun when you see it in the movies, but in reality? It's just a lot of wind, muscle strain, and panic. Maybe I screamed, I'm not sure. I do know the shock of what had happened temporarily stopped Val's crying, so—bonus?

The bridge tower loomed before us. It had four access levels connecting the spires on either side. Each level was about twenty feet wide, with only a single wire on each side to act as a railing. Plenty of space to land, if you were a member of Cirque du Soleil.

Since I was not, I simply let go of the guyline as soon as we were over the platform. I dropped about six feet, stumbled, and rolled on to my back, wrapping both arms protectively around my baby sister. Her helmet clunked against my chest as we slid to a stop, but we seemed to have avoided any massive brain traumas. I got to my feet, whooping triumphantly—

And found myself facing the third ski-masked mercenary. He stood in the doorway of the southern tower spire, backlit like a Xenomorph from the *Alien* movies. He was the one who had been scanning the bridge cable while his buddies were looking for me on the ground. I guessed he was the brains of this outfit. He was bigger than his co-killers too, with enough muscles for a whole team of Olympic weightlifters. And if his vibrating eyeballs were any indication, he had enough Fortis in his veins to kick-start the heart of an elephant.

"Very impressive," he said in a calm, creepy tone. Clearly, he'd read several chapters of *How to Skeeve People Out with Just Your Voice.* "But I'm afraid your great escape has come to an end. It's time to relinquish the child."

I snuck a glance behind me. There was an access door on the other spire, but it was a good seventy feet away. Could I run for it?

As if spotting my train of thought, Creepy Calmy pulled a MAC-10 Uzi from underneath his vest. "That, I would not recommend."

Instinctively, I spread out my hands. "You really gonna shoot a baby?" I asked him, my voice wobbling.

"I've killed more kids than measles," he said in that terrifying, emotionless tone. "Now hand her. To me."

What else could I do? My hands loosened the straps of the baby carrier. Val made a few questioning peeps as I lifted her out by the armpits. Her trusting green eyes met mine. My parents had told me babies don't remember much before the age of two, and what they do recall is positive. I really hoped that was true, because what I was about to do was pretty messed up.

"You win," I told the mercenary. I gave my sister a kiss, then rotated her body so she was facing our attacker. I slowly walked forward, holding Val out in front of me like a riot shield. "You want her? Here you go!"

Then I threw my baby sister at him.

As far back as I can remember, I wanted to be a superhero.

Naturally, my definition of the word changed a bit over the years. When I was five, I wanted to be Catboy from *PJ Masks*. At seven, I longed to turn my school principal into an underpants-wearing, monster-fighting vigilante whom only I could control. The year I turned nine, I slept over at a friend's house, and a secret, late-night viewing of Paul Verhoeven's *RoboCop* made me pray for a horrible, disfiguring accident that would make me into a bald, metal-plated cyborg.

Then at age ten, I discovered comics. For the next three years, the only superheroes I wanted to be were classic, spandex-wearing, catchphrase-spouting *superheroes*. My avatar of choice shifted on a yearly, monthly, even weekly basis, depending on which character I was currently into, but it was always someone comic-based. I didn't care whether they hailed from Marvel, DC, or the Phantom Zone—I embraced them all.

I know, I know, every kid wants to be a superhero at some point, but deep down, they know it won't really happen. Not me. The idea of gaining some superhuman ability and using it to stand out in a world that was depressing and corrupt and could ruin the *Star Wars* movies—well, that was pretty appealing to a geeky, decidedly ordinary Angeleno kid like myself. Even my name, Robbie Rampino, had the alliterative ring of a great hero's alter ego. All I needed was something that would make me special.

But up until five months ago, that cupboard was bare. I had no accidental encounters with radioactive material, no dead relatives to avenge, no out-of-control inventions for which I had to atone. My life was so boring, it wouldn't even fill three lines of an encyclopedia entry, much less a full-color, twenty-two page comic with splash pages. The only drama I had in the backstory column was that my mom died when I was six years old.

Mom and Dad met at Berkeley in the mid-nineties. They were both nerds, a fact which helped them overcome the politics that separated their families. Michael "Call Me Mike" Rampino was from the Republican suburbs of Cincinnati, Ohio; Polly Campbell was from hippy-dippy San Francisco. But they both loved pizza, indie rock, and arguing about movies. They married, got jobs at SoCal colleges, and a few years later they gave birth to me. I spent the first six years of life bingeing on the holy trifecta of American kid culture: *Sesame Street*, Nintendo, and the back catalog of Disney/Pixar.

Then my mom was diagnosed with cancer.

Honestly, I don't remember much about her before the diagnosis. She found out she had breast cancer when I was four, and after that she spent the next two years in and out of the hospital. When I think of her, I can visualize the soft curtain of her dark blond hair, her kind blue eyes, and her tired smile. She was tired all the time. Then she died, and everyone started treating me weirdly. Some adults told me I had to be a big boy now and take care of my dad, while others acted like I was the one with cancer. Kids avoided me at recess. My teachers patted my shoulder like I was made of eggshell.

Since the real world was so lame, I decided to escape it. I fed myself a steady diet of fantasy and sci-fi movies, TV, video games, and comic books. I became an expert at discussing Minecraft mobs. I memorized little-known trivia tidbits from *Wild Kratts* and *Teen Titans Go!* Anything to avoid talking about moms, cancer, or death. If my goal was to leave the ordinary behind, then I became owner, pilot, and full-time captain of the intergalactic starship *Otherworld*.

It didn't help that I grew up in one of the most white-bread cities that Southern California had to offer. Being a college town, Pasadena had an overabundance of suburban homes, chain restaurants, and seventy-five-degree, year-round sunshine. On the upside, I could ride my bike anywhere without fear of crazy drivers or criminal elements. I became a fixture at the city's great bookstores, comic book vendors, and video game sellers.

It was at one of these that I met Fletcher Grossman. We were both in sixth grade at the time, but I went to the local public middle school and he attended a fancy private place called Gates Academy. Our paths collided at Vroman's Bookstore. It was release day for the new *Injustice* comic, and our hands bumped as we both reached for the last issue on the shelf. There was a moment of silence as we faced off. Fletcher was a big kid, several inches taller than me, with thick freckled arms and a stomach that looked like he'd swallowed a BB-unit droid without chewing. He had pale pink skin, a crown of curly orange hair, and sharp blue eyes. His round belly was covered in a Marvel *Cloak & Dagger* T-shirt.

"Whoops," he said, his voice gruff and rumbly. "Guess it's not your fault you have a weakness against wood."

The random comment made me blink. "Huh?" (In my defense, I wasn't used to verbal jousting matches with strangers.)

He jerked his curly-haired noggin at my T-shirt. On the emerald-green fabric was the logo of a classic DC comics superhero—a white circle encasing two green bars with a green circle sandwiched between them. "Green Lantern?" he said, kindly leaving off the *duh*. "His weakness is wood."

"Uh, I thought it was the color yellow." He might have been bigger than me, but we were in my wheelhouse now. "His ring can't affect things that are yellow."

Fletcher's mouth twitched. Either he was pleased to find I wasn't a complete farm animal, or I'd just stepped into a trap. "Actually, the whole 'yield signs as Achilles heel' thing didn't come along until the Silver Age version. The first Green Lantern, Alan Scott, got his ring after a railroad crash. And *his* powers couldn't affect anything made of wood. Hence, my killer takedown of your spaghetti grip. Paper comic, made from wood pulp, et cetera, et cetera. Also, my dad says possession is nine-tenths of the law." He saluted me with the issue of *Injustice* and turned to leave.

"So then, you're a supervillain," I said. Fletcher paused, arching an eyebrow in my direction. "You just take whatever you want without a fair fight? Maybe I should report you to the Justice League."

He scoffed. "Like I have any respect for a group of dumb jocks who only allow one lady board member."

"Are you crazy? The JLA's had tons of women over the years. Hawkgirl, Black Canary, Vixen . . ." I hoped this might end the showdown, but Fletcher didn't bat an eye.

"But never in a leadership role. The only one who gets any respect is Wonder Woman, and that's only because no one wants to encounter the business end of her truth lasso. And do *not* get me started on her costume. Why do all the female superheroes have to wear bikinis? Superheroes are athletes—the ladies should be rocking sports bras and running pants."

"That would be like giving Iron Man a beer gut. The whole point of superheroes is that they're *super*. Physically fit. The peak of perfection."

"Which means every kid who reads comics grows up thinking muscles and hot bods are the only thing of value in the world. Just once, can we have a plus-sized, diabetic hero whose weakness is oatmeal cream pies?"

He had a point. Superman's power came from Earth's yellow sun, not lifting weights. I was amazed I'd never had this conversation before with any of my other friends. "Fair enough," I said. "From now on, I promise to only buy comics that feature regular-looking people."

Fletcher was appalled. "And miss ogling all those otherworldly hotties? Don't kill yourself over an ideal, man." He stuck the comic under his arm and held out a hand. "I'm Fletcher."

"Robbie. Robbie Rampino." We shook.

"Cool alter ego name. Tell you what. Why don't we share the *Injustice*? We can keep it at our houses on different days of the week. Like a child of divorce but without all the emotional baggage. You a milkshake fan?"

"Is Lex Luthor bald?"

"Dude. Do not get me started on the travesty that is Zack Snyder's *Batman v Superman*."

We split the cost of the *Injustice* issue and adjourned to Vroman's coffee shop, where we found we had a lot more in common than just comics. Fletcher's parents were divorced, and he lived alone with his dad, who was some big wheel in West Coast pharmaceuticals. His mom had moved to Europe fourteen months ago, so he only saw her once or twice a year. But beyond being only children who were raised by their fathers, we also liked the same TV shows and video games, as well as the same quotable movies. Even though we went to different schools, we made a point to start hanging out several days a week.

Fletcher lived in a huge mansion in Altadena. His dad was often out of town on business, so Fletcher was mostly watched over by his dad's gorilla-sized driver, Yegor, and his housekeeper/cook, Ximena. His house had a private screening room, a pool, and he owned every game console on the market, so I was happy to spend most of our hangout time there.

Going over to Fletcher's also kept me away from my own house. My dad had started dating an entertainment attorney named Brynn Cooper, and their gross flirting was tough to avoid in our small three-bedroom bungalow. But I couldn't dodge them forever. A year after they started sucking face, they sat me down to reveal something that would make it much more difficult to ignore their relationship.

"We . . . are getting married," my dad told me with an embarrassed smile.

"What what!" put in Brynn, showing off a sparkly ring.

My dad had met Brynn on a dating website. She wasn't like a wicked stepmother or anything—in fact, she had gone out of her way to be nice to me. But every time I saw her next to my dad, all I could think was, *You're not my mom.* For starters, we couldn't have looked more unrelated. Brynn had light brown skin, dark hair braided into a style she called Senegalese twists, and twinkly hazel-colored eyes that crinkled at the edges. She also liked to bake, she listened to rock music, and she played the acoustic guitar pretty well. She was fun, which was a nice contrast to my by-the-book, straitlaced dad. Frankly, I don't know what she saw in my old man.

Still, she wasn't my mom, and she never would be.

"I know I'm not your mom," she said as if overhearing my thoughts. "And I know it's going to be an adjustment, all of us living together, but I want us to be open and honest with each other, okay? You have any problems—you don't like my decorating choices, my music, my stinky feet—you come straight to me. I might be your 'stepmom,' but I want us to be friends. Cool?"

She held out her fist for a bump. It was something I didn't do even among kids my own age.

"Congratulations." I ignored her peace offering and went to my room. I knew it was rude, but my dad and I had been doing fine for six years. We didn't need some alt-rock lawyer messing up our lives.

Later that night my dad came down to my room. His beard drooped with disappointment. "Listen, Robbie. I'm always going to miss your mom. But it can't just be you and me, lone-wolfing it for the rest of our lives."

"Why not?" I said, unable to keep a childlike whine from my voice.

"Because people can't just think about themselves. There are other folks to consider, whether you like it or not. Folks like me and Brynn."

I didn't like it, but the decision had been made. Brynn moved in, and she married my dad six months later. They spent two weeks in the British Isles for their honeymoon, while I stayed at Fletcher's place, playing video games and binge-watching *Battlestar Galactica* (both versions).

Four months after that, they sat me down for another awkward dinner, only this time they told me that Brynn was pregnant. They'd been trying since before the wedding (gross) and she was clearly over the moon to be a biological mother.

Me, I couldn't care less. I'd just turned twelve, and I'd gotten used to the freedom that came with being an only child. If I didn't want to do some family activity, we tended not to do it. I also knew one or two classmates who'd recently had younger siblings, and they all seemed to resent them in some way. Six months later, I learned why.

Valeria Ruth Cooper Rampino was born on Friday, September 13. She was eight pounds of curly brown hair, squishy beige skin, bright hazel eyes, and a seriously strong set of lungs. The kid could scream. And scream. And when she was done with that, she'd scream some more.

The first three months of Val's life were a blur of baby barf, smelly diapers, and sleep deprivation. Newborns don't do much, but she still managed to take up a lot of my dad and Brynn's time. Swaddling, bottle warmers, nursing holds, umbilical cord care, cradle cap, colic— these topics were all they talked about. All the while, a near-endless parade of relatives and visitors passed through the house, doing nothing but coo at the baby. Even my grandparents ignored me.

But eventually our house adjusted to the exhaustion, and my dad and Brynn began to get a grip on parenting. Brynn went back to her job at the law firm, hiring a twenty-two-year-old college grad named Shelby to watch the baby during the day. They tried to encourage me to hang out with Val, but honestly, once you get past the cuteness, babies are pretty boring. Sure, I gave her the occasional bottle—I'm not a total monster—but that was pretty much the limit to our interactions until I finished eighth grade and went on summer break.

With all the fuss over the new baby, I had managed to avoid being signed up for the usual lame summer camps my dad chose for me. Three months of blank, blissfully empty calendar squares stretched out before me. The first couple weeks of vacation were everything I hoped they would be. I'd sleep in till ten or so, eat breakfast, say adios to Shelby and the baby, then spend the rest of the day goofing off with Fletcher, while Yegor drove us wherever we wanted to go. It was quickly shaping up to be the Best Summer Ever.

Then, in the third week of my summer vacay, just a few days after her nine-month birthday, I discovered my half sister's superpower.

The whole thing started with a bag of Cool Ranch Doritos.

It wasn't my fault it happened. After that first chapter, you probably think I'm one of those big brothers who leaves his kid sis outside in one-hundred-degree heat while he plays Fortnite inside the air-conditioned house. I'll admit, there were times I was certainly capable of something like that. I was a thirteen-year-old boy—babysitting, even for my own sister, was pretty far down on my list of priorities. And whether Brynn and my dad picked up on this, or they just didn't trust me, I'd never been asked to watch Val by myself.

But on the day in question, Brynn and my dad had tickets to the Emmy Awards. They'd only had a few nights out on their own since Val had been born, so when one of Brynn's clients offered her the seats, they jumped at the chance to party like celebs. Then Shelby texted them a couple hours before they were about to leave, telling them she'd eaten something "janky" and now her stomach was going "cray-cray." She even added a barfing emoji so they'd know how serious it was. They began scrambling to find a replacement, but so far had come up empty.

"Who else can we call?" Brynn asked, pacing back and forth in our small kitchen. Her hair was pinned up above her head in a complicated swoop and she wore a sparkly blue cocktail dress. Val sat in her high chair, chucking Cheerios on the floor, while I calmly ate my lunch. "I don't want some first-time sitter we've never met," she added.

My dad scrolled through the contacts in his phone. "This is worse than the Super Bowl. Everyone we know is booked."

"The show starts in forty minutes," my stepmom said, checking the time on her phone. "There's gotta to be someone we trust who could watch Val."

They both turned to me in slow motion. "Oh, no," I said, putting down my quesadilla. "I've never watched her by myself before. I don't even know how to change a diaper."

"Easiest thing in the world," said my dad. "Zip, zap, wipe. We're talking one, two diapers, tops."

"What about food?" I protested.

"You've given her bottles before," said Brynn. "There's formula in the fridge, and squeezy pouches if she's still hungry."

"And if she chokes? I don't know the Baby Heimlich."

"Just tilt her over and give her a couple whacks on the back," said my dad. "That doesn't work, call 911." He was already pulling on his suit jacket.

"This is incredibly irresponsible," I informed them. "And unfair. I was gonna go hang out at Fletcher's today."

Brynn put in her earrings, using the toaster as a mirror. "Have him come over here for once. He can help. 'Two Teens and a Baby'—that sounds fun, right?"

My dad took me by the shoulders. "You're thirteen now, Robbie. For a few hours, we're asking you to be the man of the house. You have to take part in this family sometime."

Before I could argue, Brynn swooped in to kiss me on the cheek.

"You're our hero, honey. Emergency numbers are on the fridge. Just text us if you have any questions."

I wiped her lipstick off my cheek. "Fine. But if anything happens, it's on you guys."

"Have fun!" said my dad. Then they were gone, in a flurry of air kisses and perfume.

I looked at my half sister, scowling. "You better not wreck my afternoon."

"Wah oooh," she replied.

* * *

It was only an hour or so after my parents left, however, that she upended a lot more than my plans. Fletcher hadn't shown up yet, so I decided to change Val's diaper before putting her down for her nap. Thankfully, it wasn't a poopy one. She weighed barely eighteen pounds, but the kid could drop a deuce like a three-hundred-pound trucker after a chili-eating contest.

I had just cinched a fresh diaper around Val's chubby legs and set her on the floor when I got a text from Fletcher. It was a video link, with an attached message: *Check it out, dood!!*

I tapped on the link. The video was taken from the body cam of a Florida police officer. A banner at the bottom said *ZOMBIE OR SUPERVILLAIN? WARNING—GRAPHIC CONTENT!* The cop crept around the corner of a convenience store, his gun at the ready, to see a wiry man punching holes in the brick wall surrounding an ATM. He was muscled, with a military tattoo on his left shoulder and a jarhead-style haircut.

"Sir, please stop hitting the wall," the police officer said in a nervous, shaky voice. "And slowly put your hands in the air."

Brick Fists turned to him, panting like he'd just run a marathon. His pupils were like two large black marbles, and they were vibrating.

Blood dripped from his obviously broken knuckles, but the guy didn't seem to care.

"I said grab some sky, or I will shoot." But Brick Fists started shuffling forward. The officer fired—*bam bam bam*—and three red spots appeared in the crazy guy's tank top. He touched one of the bloody holes with a bent finger and smiled. Then he leapt forward like a crazed animal—

And the body cam cut to black. Video over.

Yawn, I texted back. *Solid CG, but been there, done that.* I hit send and ripped open a bag of Cool Ranch Doritos.

Now, before I describe what happened next, you should be aware of a couple things. First, Val had pulled herself up to sitting once or twice before, but at that point she couldn't stand or crawl. All she could do consistently was roll over, and that was pretty well telegraphed with lots of moans and grunting. Secondly, I had made sure to set her on an area of the floor that had no circus cannons or catapult-like contraptions within reach. So what transpired next was entirely her doing.

The sound of the ripping bag startled her, and her chubby feet kicked off the floor. She flew upward like a helium balloon, six or seven feet straight off the ground. I watched her ascent, too surprised to move. There was a terrible, century-spanning moment of silence . . .

Then she dropped back down, and hit the hardwood floor.

Maybe I closed my eyes. Maybe my heart stopped. A thousand scary images exploded in my brain. Me, rushing Val into an emergency room. A baby-sized spinal column, snapping like a stalk of celery. Christopher Reeve in his wheelchair. Other celebrities in wheelchairs. Stephen Hawking scowling at me, his robot voice intoning, *The human race finds you guilty of being a bad brother.*

But then, a miracle.

There was no cry of pain, no crack of bone, no wet *splosh* of brains.

Instead she bounced.

And not some kind of "left fielder diving for a catch and face-planting in the outfield" bounce. I'm talking a fully synthetic, Looney Tunes–style, Super Ball–grade recoil. It was even accompanied by an actual cartoon *boing*.

Val popped back up into the air, upside down and giggling.

She hung before me for a beat, a period on a Spanish question mark, until gravity began to pull her back to earth. My hands shot out, grabbing my baby sister firmly around the waist before she could hit the floor again. I turned her right side up. Val waved her arms, gurgling in pleasure.

I quickly placed her on the dresser changing pad, tummy side down, as if she were a chunk of hot uranium. Gently, I prodded her skull and neck. There were no bumps, dents, contusions, not even a discoloration. Somehow my sister had struck a hardwood floor from a height of six feet, bounced, and emerged completely unscathed.

I rolled Val on her back and peered at her eyes. I had heard you should check a kid's eyes after a fall, but I had forgotten what I was supposed to be looking for. Blood? Dilated pupils? Disapproval? A quick consultation with Dr. Google revealed the size of her pupils should be the same. They were.

"Are you okay?" I asked her in disbelief. "How are you okay?"

In response, Val gave me a big toothless grin.

* * *

"Dude, she's fine," said Fletcher. We were sitting in the living room, thirty minutes after Val's logic-defying display. He lifted my baby sister off the rug, inspecting her with mock seriousness. Fletcher still had the same boyish, excitable energy he'd possessed when I first met him, but late-night snacks and a hatred of exercise had led to him putting on some weight. His vintage *Voltron: Defender of the Universe* shirt was stretched near to ripping across his round belly. "You're sure she bounced?"

"Like a basketball on the moon," I said. "I know, I sometimes have a tendency to exaggerate things, but this? Was the craziest thing I've ever seen. And it was *real.*"

"Maybe baby bones are more flexible than adults'," he suggested. "And all this squish makes her a bouncing baby girl. Right, squishy? Right?" He tickled Val's belly, making her laugh.

"What if she's got some weird bone disorder?" I countered. "Like, they're hollow, or rubber, or . . ."

"Or you're just guilty she got a boo-boo on your first time babysitting." He made faces at the baby. "But you're fine, aren't you? Aren't you, baby girl? Yes!"

"Exactly. That's why this is so weird!"

"What do you want me to say? You're lucky you got lucky." He passed Val back to me. "Now let's play *Fortnite* so I can pwn some noobs." *Pwn* rhymed with *cone,* and for Fletcher the term meant "defeat with as much humiliation as possible." He was a much better gamer than most people (me included), so inventing complicated elims was the only way he could keep things interesting for himself.

But I wasn't ready to change topics yet. "You think it was luck? Watch this." I set my baby sister on the dining room table, took a step back, and ripped open another bag of chips.

Boing. Val's eyes went wide and she launched off the table, going skyward like a fresh-from-the-can racquetball. When she started to drop, I stepped forward and caught her in my arms. The baby laughed.

Fletcher laughed too. "Sweet. How'd you do that, concealed bungee cords? Airbag in her diaper? Come on, I promise I won't post your trick on TikTok."

"It's not a trick," I said, passing him my sister. "Feel her legs. There's no pads or wires or anything."

As he obliged me, I walked into the kitchen and got another bag of chips. "Yes, I confirm there are no wires or hidden pads," he said in an unimpressed robot voice. "So, is this, like, part two of the trick, or—what the freak!"

Val reacted as I opened the new chip bag. She shot out of Fletcher's arms, ricocheted off the dining room wall, bounced against the ceiling, and landed back in my arms, unhurt. She squealed, swinging her hands as if we were playing a fun game.

My friend stared. "Okay, that—how in the name of Voldemort did you do that?"

"It's happened, like, six times now," I told him. "I'm freaking out."

"Do it again," Fletcher said. I hesitated. "Come on, you wanna figure out how it works, right?"

I complied, opening my seventh bag of chips for the day and surprising my baby sister. She bounced off the hardwood floor, swinging her chubby fists like she was swimming. I caught her under the arms and set her in her jungle seat. This was a plastic chair with lots of attachments to stimulate her mushy infant mind. She screeched, pressing buttons and pulling knobs as if it were her job.

Fletcher's face got serious. "Do you swear you're not messing with me? Swear it. Swear on the ghost of Jack Kirby that you are not messing with me."

"I'm not messing with you," I said, pacing back and forth anxiously. "I showed you this 'cause I need help! What should I do here? There's no baby website for stuff like this. If I show my parents, they'll probably have her locked up."

Fletcher joined me in my pacing. "Definitely do not tell any more people," he said. "Especially your parents. We need to keep this quiet."

"But something's *wrong* with her. My baby sister's a—" The words *freak*, *anomaly*, and *monstrosity* appeared in my head. I tried to ignore them. "She's sick. Or something. We need to run some tests, get a

CAT scan. Or an exorcist. 'Cause that—she—is not normal."

"You're right," he said. A big grin began to spread across his freckled face. "She's not normal at all."

"So what then? Why are you smiling?"

"Because, dude," he said, looking happier than I'd ever seen him. "Your sister? Has a *superpower.*"

Gates Academy stood on a hill just off Mulholland Drive. The campus of Fletcher's school was like something out of an *X-Men* movie. A thick eight-foot hedge surrounded the perimeter. The buildings inside were brick and stone, with iron-webbed glass windows, making the place look more like an Ivy League college than a private school. Perfectly manicured pebble paths and fairway-smooth grass lawns connected the half dozen buildings. On a clear day, you could see all the way to the ocean. The class roster of the academy was like a Who's Who for Gifted Kids of Wealthy Parents. It was also a nontraditional school, so among other features, students had access to the facilities year-round.

That last part was why Fletcher and I were able to come here on a Saturday afternoon in June. After a lengthy debate about what exactly constituted a "superpower" (final consensus: anything inorganic, manufactured, or easily used by someone else did not count), we decided we needed a third opinion. As I'd already said, my parents would freak if we showed them what Val could do. My school friends would just want to take videos and post them on YouTube. My neighbors would probably call the cops. We needed someone who could be objective. Who wouldn't want to take advantage of my sister. Someone, we decided, with a background in science, who had access to science-y equipment.

"I got it," Fletcher had said after we'd named and discarded eight or nine unrealistic candidates. "We'll call Mousehands."

This was his uncharitable nickname for Patty Nakong, an eighth-grade girl he knew from Gates Academy. There had been a "will they, won't they" simmer between them a few months back, and they seemed to have a lot in common, but eventually Fletcher decided her "small pink hands looked too much like mouse paws." I suspected it was really because he didn't like hanging out with someone smarter than he was.

"You really think she'll help us?" I asked. "I mean, you were kind of a jerk to her." Fletcher had asked Patty to the academy's Valentine's dance, then spent most of the time hanging out with his guy friends.

"That was months ago. I'm sure she's gotten over that." He was already scrolling through his phone contacts. "Patty Cakes," he said in a sleazy purr when she picked up. How he convinced any girls to go to any dances with him was beyond me. "Are you at that dorky science camp yet?"

"It's a genetics camp, and it starts in August," Patty said. From the tone of her voice, it sounded like her definition of "getting over" something differed greatly from Fletcher's. "What do you want?"

He gave me a thumbs-up. "What's your afternoon look like? My friend Robbie and I are working on this, uh, new project, and we'd love to meet up at the Gates lab to discuss it. Maybe borrow some of your science-y know-how?" We had agreed that telling her about Val's superpower over the phone might not be the best way to get her assistance.

After some hemming and hawing, she grudgingly agreed to meet with us. So now, forty minutes later, Fletcher and I were traversing the ridiculously gorgeous grounds of Gates Academy. Yegor, as usual, had stayed behind in the car. I pushed Val in her stroller while she nommed on her favorite toy, a squeezy white giraffe.

The science lab was located in a three-story modern art sculpture located at the center of campus. Fletcher told me the whole building had been paid for by some eccentric Silicon Valley CEO, and it showed. Polished steel and tempered glass swooped around each other like a flash-frozen tornado of building materials. Solar panels were placed on every available surface, automatically rotating to catch the most sun. We took the elevator down to the basement, where an electronic lock buzzed us into a high-tech, top-of-the-line science lab. A short, scowling Vietnamese girl turned to greet us. She had a black-haired bowl cut that covered her head and ears like a swimming cap, and oversized square-framed glasses that made her look a lot like Velma from *Scooby-Doo*. The only thing missing was an orange turtleneck under her lab coat.

"Patty, dahling," Fletcher said in a terrible British accent. "Are you a Large Hadron Collider? 'Cause you look smashing."

He tried to go in for a hug, but she stopped him with a hand to the face. "I had to beg my mom to pay for my Lyft ride here, so skip to the part where you tell me what you want."

"Are we alone?" I asked. The campus had seemed pretty empty when we walked through it, but I wanted to make sure some janitor wouldn't barge in on us.

"It's summer," she said. "I've been coming here to help Dr. Suresh with his research, but we're practically the only ones around. We won't be bothered."

"Perfect," I said. "We need to keep this quiet." I quickly explained everything that had occurred so far, ending with a demonstration of Val's bouncing ability. To Patty's credit, she merely readjusted her glasses before asking me to demonstrate.

"Fascinating," she said after I startled and then caught my bouncing sister. Patty pulled on a rubber glove and poked Val's chubby legs. You gotta hand it to science-y types. Something that would send normal people running for the angry mob torches makes the lab coats actually lean forward in curiosity. Patty looked up at me, her dark brown eyes shining. "You mind if I run some tests?"

"Some" turned out to be an understatement. Over the next two hours, Patty prodded, poked, examined, scanned, and recorded every measurement on my sister imaginable. She took Val's weight, height, body fat index, skin samples, and DNA. She checked her eyesight, her hearing, her sense of smell, and her response to flavored taste bud strips. We only took a break to change Val's poopy diaper, and even that was of interest to the budding geneticist, who dubbed the baby's waste "invaluable data."

But the most important test came when she brushed Val's arm with a pad of steel wool. Tiny crackles of blue lightning sparked off my baby sister's skin, then disappeared. Patty went to find a device called an electrometer, which was basically a metal rod plugged into a meter display. She passed the wand over the baby's body, hmming and nodding as the meter jumped up and down. Patty set aside the electrometer, then suddenly jumped in front of Val.

"Boo!" she said. There was that familiar *boing*, and Val bounced upward. At the same time, Patty's metal glasses popped off her face. I rushed forward to catch my sister. She squealed happily.

"How 'bout a little warning next time?" I said, placing the baby back in her stroller.

"Sorry," Patty said brightly. "But surprising her was necessary for my diagnosis."

Fletcher was brandishing a couple of test tubes like nunchucks. "So you know what's up with her, then?"

She took the fragile glass tubes out of his hands. "Well, she's perfectly healthy."

"You mean, except for the bouncing," I said.

"It's not bouncing," she said, placing the tubes back in their metal rack. "It's magnetism."

I blinked. "Like . . . she's super-charming?"

Patty rubbed her own arm with the steel wool. "No, actual magnetism. Every animal generates an electromagnetic field. Humans don't get much from theirs except the occasional doorknob shock." She held a finger near a metal test tube rack, producing a small electric spark. "Other animals, though, can actually control their EM fields. Some use them for navigation, some can zap predators, but it appears Val is using hers as a sort of protective reflex. She gets startled, cranks up her EM field, and repels herself away from danger. Hence, the 'bouncing.'"

"Told you, dude," said Fletcher proudly. "She's an X-Man."

Patty wrinkled her nose. "I'm sure, once her condition is granted an official name, it will be something more gender-neutral."

"I don't care about the name," I said. "I just want to know that she's . . . that this is really . . . You're sure she wasn't zapped with an Infinity Gem or imbued with the Power Cosmic or something?"

Patty stared at me. "I don't know what those things are, but they sound very unscientific."

"But you said it's a condition. Can she control it?" I said.

Patty shrugged. "Probably. Right now she's using it instinctively. But humans are born with a bunch of reflexes—sucking, gripping, pooping—that we later learn to control. At least, most of us do." She gave Fletcher a withering glance.

The big guy began pacing with excitement. "Think of all the cool crap she's gonna be able to do. Flip cars, stop bullets, fly—"

"We don't know that she can do any of that," Patty interrupted. "What we need are more tests. CAT scans, MRIs, a full genetic screening. Procedures I can't do on my own. We need to determine how she controls her EM field, how strong it is . . . and most important, whether it could hurt her." She turned to me. "Obviously, you'll have to tell your parents."

"Whoa, whoa, whoa," said Fletcher. "I'm all for keeping the baby safe, but you know what's gonna happen if we bring adults in on this. They're gonna take Val away and lock her in some CIA black site for the rest of her life."

"If you want to determine the extent of her power and how to control it," said Patty, "then maybe that's best. Val needs to be studied."

They both looked at me for a decision. "All this . . . it's a lot to take in," I replied. "I want to keep her safe, but I also don't want her becoming some lab rat for the government. I think . . . we have to think it over."

Patty looked disappointed, but she took it well. "Of course. She's your sister, and it's a big choice. I'll just keep all this Nobel Prize–winning data under wraps until you decide. Not like anyone would believe me anyway." She pointed at Fletcher. "However. Until we fully catalog her abilities, she might react in unexpected, potentially harmful ways. Don't do anything dumb without telling me, okay?"

"Patty Cakes, what do you take us for?" said Fletcher, throwing a thick arm around her. "We're both 'safety first' kind of guys."

She shrugged off his arm. "I know exactly what kind of guy you are. Which is why I said it."

I rubbed a hand on Val's soft, fuzzy head. At that moment, it was hard to imagine such a cute pile of cinnamon squoosh could do anything remotely harmful or unexpected.

She would prove me wrong less than two hours later.

"The Diaper Duo."

"Magnet Girl."

"Lone Wolf and Chubbs."

"Electronica."

"Bouncy Belle."

"EM-She."

I snarfed my lemonade. Fletcher and I were walking down the Santa Monica Pier, finishing off a handheld dinner from Hot Dog on a Stick. The pier was a big tourist trap, lined with restaurants, souvenir shops, amusement park rides, and a 130-foot-tall Ferris wheel. It could be a pretty annoying place to deal with, people-wise, but after spending the last few hours in the Gates Academy basement, doing every kind of boring scientific measurement there was, I wanted to be outside among real, uncomplicated humanity. Yegor was twenty feet behind us, his ice-blond polar bear hulk encased in a black suit and sunglasses. His face was as impassive as always. Fletcher had bragged that his driver used to be a KGB operative, and for once I was inclined to believe him.

Val was strapped to my chest in her baby carrier. It had taken me and Fletcher several minutes to figure out how to get her into it, and Yegor had refused to help us. "I drive," he said in his thick Russian bear-growl. "I do not sit with baby."

Eventually we managed to cram Val against my chest and make sure she was secure. A good thing, too—it was a lot easier navigating the pier crowds with a baby carrier instead of a stroller. Val had fallen asleep during the drive down from Gates Academy and was still a little groggy, but the sight of the sparkling ocean was beginning to perk her up. I had cinched a floppy white hat on her head to protect her eyes from the western sun.

I blew my nose on a napkin, expelling the last of the lemonade from my sinuses. "Please do not demean my sister with your name suggestions. No 'girl,' 'lady,' 'She-something,' 'blank-ette,' or anything that insults her gender."

It was against my better judgment that we were even having this conversation. Once the initial excitement over Val's ability had worn off, Fletcher immediately started campaigning for superhero names. At first I had refused to participate, but soon it became too much of a fun game to ignore.

He took a bite of his pretzel dog. "You're the one trying to latch onto her hero identity," he said with his mouth full. "Val's the one with powers. At best, you could be her sidekick. What do you think, baby girl? You want your big bro to be your sidekicky-wicky?" He tickled her under the chin, a move that was always good for a gurgle. "See? She agrees with me. So quit trying to horn in on her talent and be the Alfred to her Batman." He took a triumphant slurp of his lemonade.

"This is stupid. She can't even walk or talk yet."

"The future begins today, dude. Eventually she's gonna be out there, by herself, bing-boinging off supervillains left and right. She needs a name that will stand with her. Something simple. Striking. Too bad Supergirl's already taken."

"Uh, no, it's not," I said. "Did you miss my previous point about demeaning names?"

"Superwoman, then. Superbaby? Superkid!"

"We're not calling her 'Super' anything, because she's not fighting crime." I readjusted Val's hat so the afternoon sun was out of her eyes. "You know why there aren't any superheroes in the real world? Because they all get killed. Anyone with power—Abe Lincoln, Martin Luther King, Joan of Arc—*kkkcchh*." I swiped a finger across my throat.

"Wrong. There aren't any superheroes because *no one* can do what Val can. If some nutjob tried to shoot her, the bullet would probably just bounce off!"

"That's a big probably," I said. "And I don't particularly want to test that theory in Patty's lab to see if it's true. This has been fun, but we're done, man."

"Done? Done?! She's nine months old. We haven't even started!"

"Exactly." I crumpled my lemonade cup, pretending it was my dreams. "You think I don't want to be her sidekick? Help people, change the world, be the star of my own real-life comic? I would *kill* for that. But I can't let her get hurt."

"That's the beauty of her power. It *protects* her. And you heard what Patty said: it's only gonna get stronger and crazier as she grows up. You don't deal with it now, who knows how she'll use it once she can walk and talk!"

"What do you want me to do? Call up S.H.I.E.L.D.? Enroll her in Professor X's School for Gifted Youngsters? Those things don't *exist*." Hearing the tension in our voices, Val moaned. I rubbed her back to show I wasn't angry with her.

"So we'll do it ourselves. Figure out her strengths, her weaknesses, train her . . . classic origin story stuff. This thing she can do, it's incredible. More than that, it's a *gift*. With great power . . . you know the rest."

"I can't believe you just quoted *Spider-Man* to me."

"Dude, it's the best one of the franchise."

"Better than *Homecoming*? Now I know you're crazy."

We stopped near the end of the pier. About ninety feet below, waves crashed against the barnacle-crusted pylons. This far offshore, the water was pretty deep. A handful of surfers were daring one another to ride the swells through the gauntlet of wooden poles beneath us.

Fletcher gripped the wooden railing with his pale freckled hands. "You can't ignore this, buddy. What you have, it's, like, a once-in-a-lifetime thing. Once-in-a-million lifetimes." My best friend was not, as a rule, an earnest guy. Hearing him talk in such an open, pleading way was almost scarier than the thought of Val getting injured. I realized he must have wanted to be a superhero as much as I did. Maybe more. Still . . .

"What if she gets hurt?" I asked. "You've read comics—every time anyone tries to do some good, a villain shows up to screw them over. I'm not Alfred, and I'm definitely not Bruce Wayne. I don't have a Batcave and ninja training and a bajillion dollars to protect her."

"So we'll take precautions. We'll keep our identities secret, do everything over the Internet. Buy body armor."

I couldn't help riffing with him a little. "I did hear about this app that can disguise your IP address."

"And if we need money, we can take donations," he said. "Set up a . . . GoFundMe or something. People would love throw virtual tips at a superhero. Actually, screw donations—corporate sponsors are where the real money's at. Pampers would be all over Superbaby."

"I told you, we're not going with that name. But yeah, it is weird that no superheroes have sponsors. One Nike check mark on Spider-Man's costume, and he'd be out of debt in no time. Or Little Caesars."

I adopted a 1950s announcer voice. "'This bad guy capture brought to you by your friendly neighborhood chicken alfredo pizza.'"

"Aquaman Cruise Ships."

"Wonder Woman Airlines."

Fletcher's phone buzzed. Probably an update from one of the many geeky message boards he was on. While he typed a quick response, Val burbled and pointed at the ocean, reminding me what we were really talking about here. "How do we train a baby?" I asked. "She can't even feed herself."

He hit send and re-pocketed his phone. "We'll take it slow. You think Supes was flying before he could walk?"

It was a cute image, but it also made me realize something. "We are in such uncharted territory here. I can't even think of a comic book that deals with baby superpowers, much less a real-world organization."

"Oonee wanna," Val agreed.

I rested my chin on top of her soft head. She smelled of milk, Hawaiian rolls, and responsibility. "And if we were to do anything, how would we keep it a secret? This isn't like staying up past our bedtimes. If my parents find out—"

"HELP! SOMEBODY HELP!"

The cry came from a teenage girl farther down the pier. She was pointing at the water below, frantically trying to grab everyone's attention. Fletcher and I leaned over the railing. Ninety feet beneath us, a man in a flannel shirt and jeans floated facedown in the water.

"He's drowning!" the girl continued. "Someone call a lifeguard!"

Several people were already on their cell phones or waving down security, but it was obvious there was no one in the nearby water who could help. The closest surfers were at least fifty yards closer to shore, and the nearest lifeguard tower was all the way down at the beach. One of Baywatch's finest dove into the water, but Fletcher articulated what we were all thinking:

"He's never gonna make it in time. Somebody has to jump."

He looked at me.

"Oh, no," I said. "No, no, no. Are you nuts? It's, like, a hundred feet."

"It's eighty, max." He lowered his voice. "Val will protect you."

"How? She thinks her hand is food!" My sister was indeed nomming her fist like it was a candy apple.

"Magnetism," he said. "When you drop, she'll do her protective-magnet-instinct thing. You grab the guy and paddle to shore."

"He's sinking!" the girl cried. "Oh my God, he's gonna die!"

Fletcher nudged me toward the railing. "Stop it!" I whispered. "I've never taken a water rescue class, Val doesn't know how to swim, and, and . . . I don't even have a way to hide our identities."

He dumped the half-eaten pretzel dog from his Hot Dog on a Stick bag and poked two holes in it. It did reasonably pass for a superhero mask.

"She can do this," he urged me. "And so can you, dude. You gonna let that guy drown?"

"Arrgh." Making sure Yegor wasn't watching, I grabbed the fast food bag and pulled it over my head. My nose was blanketed in a fog of deep-fried fast-food grease. I looked over the railing. It was a long way down to the water. I double-checked Val's straps. The guy floated almost directly below us.

"No way," I said. "It's too—"

Then Fletcher popped a bag of potato chips.

Val startled. There was a *boing*, and we both shot up into the air.

"Is that a baby?" I heard someone say.

Then we began to drop. We plummeted past the pier. As we fell, Fletcher called after me: "Remember to support her heeeeaaaad!"

The fall felt a lot farther than ninety feet. My heart took the express elevator up my esophagus. The rushing wind made it impossible for me to hear anything other than my own mental screams. I tried to straighten my legs so we'd hit the water feetfirst. I figured if Olympic high divers could do it, maybe I had a chance at survival. Should I point my toes, though, or keep them flat? I realized it wouldn't matter either way if my legs were shattered.

Thankfully, I didn't have to find out. Fifteen feet from the water, there was another high-pitched, twangy *boing*. Our suicidal descent slowed to the speed of a dandelion puff out for a Sunday stroll. On the pier above, I could hear gasps and some exclamations of disbelief.

"Holy crap, you can fly?" I asked my baby sister. "You can *fly!*"

Val squealed, waving her arms in excitement. Technically, what she was doing was more akin to floating, but still—we were two human beings thumbing our noses at gravity, coasting through air on nothing more than my sister's superpowered magnetism. It was everything I had been dreaming of since the day I had cracked open my first comic book. I flung out my arms and closed my eyes, imaging that I was soaring above the earth. It felt *amazing*.

Then my feet touched the cold water of the Pacific, and I remembered where I was. I scanned the water, seeing the guy was still floating facedown, twenty-five feet to our left. Make that twenty-six feet. Twenty-seven. What the heck? Somehow we were gently being nudged sideways. I tried to course correct, but there's a reason more birds aren't shaped like sea stars. The aerodynamics suck. I pinwheeled my arms through the air, but it had about as much effect as propelling an eighty-foot luxury yacht with a handful of Kleenex.

"Any chance you can magnetize thataway?" I said to Val.

"Onna burbee," she replied, then blew a raspberry.

"You need me to startle you or something? Okay." I clapped my hands and wiggled my fingers in front of her face. "Boo. Blah. RAWR!"

This last word had the desired effect. But instead of moving toward the drowning guy, we *boing*-ed straight upward, twenty or thirty feet off the water. I could hear people on the pier gasp.

"Bad baby!" I said. "Down, down, go back down."

We began to drop again, but this time it was more of a gradual descent. Within seconds we had reached the water. My toes dipped into the cold Pacific, which immediately soaked through my gray Converse. I kicked my legs, slowly paddling us toward the guy. We continued to slowly sink, until the chilly ocean water was halfway up my thighs. The good news was, we were now within grabbing distance of Flannel Guy. The bad news? It felt like a hundred icicles were jabbing into my legs and buttocks. Why did the Pacific have to be so freezing? I attempted to ignore the cold, and clutched the back of the dude's shirt. I rolled him over, revealing a nasty, bleeding gash on his forehead. Water dribbled from his mouth, and his blue goateed face made him look like Hippie Smurf. I tried to pull him toward me, but have you ever deadlifted a 160-pound unconscious lump with a baby attached to your chest? Take it from me, it's not easy.

"Hey, buddy," I gently shook him. "YO." There was no response, so I shook him harder. "You're about to win the Darwin award here, wake up."

No dice. I had just managed to grab his ankle when Val's bare feet touched the water. Now, my sister has never liked baths. My parents had tried various temperatures, washing her in the sink, even sponging her down. Every time, she acted like they were bathing her in acid.

So when her chubby toes touched the ice-cold Pacific, Val reacted as if she'd been dipped in a volcano. Her legs jerked upward, and her face screwed up into the silent precursor of a crying fit. Her cinnamon-colored limbs began to vibrate with rage. I hooked Flannel Guy's foot through one of the baby carrier straps just as Val shot skyward, taking me and the unconscious man with her.

The straps of the carrier nearly dislocated both of my shoulders, but the guy stayed where he was, dangling upside down from my waist like a fish on a hook. We continued to rise upward, but the extra weight seemed to slow Val's terror-inspired moon shot. She kicked and wailed in anger.

"Hey. You listen to me, young lady." We were fifty feet off the water now, and still climbing. "If you don't demagnetize right now, I'm gonna—whoa!"

Her ascent took on another burst of speed. So much for trying to threaten a nine-month-old. Val strained against the baby carrier and flapped her arms. The heel of the surfer was starting to feel like a red-hot poker digging into my side.

Val's electromagnetic field carried us past the Santa Monica Pier. The crowd cheered as we sailed by, but I was too busy trying to adjust Flannel Guy's Ankle Bone of Pain to strike a heroic pose. Did I mention I wasn't exactly in top physical shape? The biggest object I'd ever lifted before now was Fletcher, and that was a one-second dare. The lifeless bag of bones currently dangling from the baby carrier was at least fifty bills heavier, and I wouldn't be able to cut him loose anytime soon. Yet my dumb half sister was the one doing all the complaining.

I tried a different tack. "It's okay, sweetie. We're okay." I made my voice as soothing as possible, which is hard to do when you're being gored in the side. "This really hurts, but I'm not mad. Not if you take us down. Can you do 'down'? Down?"

Another gust of wind pushed us toward the shore just south of the pier. A few people on the beach were already taking note of our approach, pointing and snapping pics with their camera phones. Even from the depths of my discomfort, I realized the importance of a photo op. I tried to strike a dashing, comic book pose, bending one knee and pointing the other leg back, like I was leaping to the rescue. It was not a pleasant feeling.

Val's cries transitioned to soft, moaning hiccups. At the same time, Flannel Guy coughed, spitting up ocean water. I guess being inverted was having some good effects. He bucked and flailed, which, hooray for his survival, but boo for the thirteen-year-old kid trying to keep him from dropping a hundred feet to the ocean.

"Chill out, man!" I said. "You passed out in the water and we're here to rescue you."

"Who . . . who are you, bro?" he said.

Fletcher was right: having an official hero name would have been so boss right then. Instead I said, "Ummm . . . I'll get back to you on that. Just stop kicking."

He strained his head up to get a better look at us, and got an eyeful of my baby sister's bare feet. "What the hell is that?!"

"That's my sister," I said proudly. "And she just saved your life, so let's watch the potty mouth, huh?"

Val seemed to realize we were getting closer to shore, because her

EM field began to decrease. By the time we reached the beach, we were only a few feet off the ground. Flannel Guy's head touched sand, and I finally was able to unhook his foot from the baby carrier. While he rolled across the beach, Val and I touched down a few feet past him, stumbling only slightly. Not bad for our first landing.

"Good job, sweetie," I said, kissing her head. "And you," I continued, turning to our goateed rescuee. I deepened my voice to what I hoped was superhero range. "No more goofing around underneath the pier, huh? That's how people get killed."

I gave him an awkward salute and jogged off. I'd have to work on my exit lines.

A few people trailed after us, but farther up the beach there was a playground and open-air gymnastic area. It was crowded with bystanders watching a few acrobatic show-off performers, so I was able to ditch the Hot Dog on a Stick bag and slip back onto the pier. As I wiped corn dog grease off my nose, Fletcher came running down to meet us. He was panting and his T-shirt was soaked with multiple sweat puddles. Yegor trailed behind him, looking completely unimpressed by what he'd witnessed in the last half hour. My friend, however, was beside himself with fanboy excitement.

"That. Was. Amaze-balls! I mean, when she took off over the pier? It was like when he catches the helicopter in *Superman*, only you guys did it for realsies!! You're superheroes! Actual, real-life *superheroes!*"

"Well, I don't feel very super," I said. "I think that guy broke my back muscles."

"Who cares? People are flipping, dude. Everyone's been waiting their whole lives to see something like that."

I couldn't help grinning. "Really? You think anyone got it on camera?"

Fletcher's smile grew even wider, until I worried it might crack his face in half. "Oh, they did a little more than that."

Nobody knows why something goes viral. Sure, there have been all kinds of studies made, and there are certainly some key factors shared by each Internet flavor of the week. Whether it's a video, tweet, meme, picture, or article, the thing has to be simple. It has to be relatable, it has to be unique, and it has to have some click-worthy quality that makes people want to spread it like the plague. This last factor is the real mystery. It can't be quantified, purchased, predicted, or created. If it could, everything thrown online would nab a hundred million views.

But before you can get even one view, you need that thing. Ours, as it turned out, was a video. Twenty-three people had caught Val's superpowered Santa Monica rescue on camera. Two-thirds of them were phone pictures—blurry, pixelated, Bigfoot-quality shots that were pretty much useless as evidence—but six were in full video. One armchair cinematographer even happened to be on the pier with his high-end Canon digital camera. Once the cry for help had drawn his attention, the guy (Señor_Muybridge was his YouTube handle) started recording. He'd managed to capture the entire rescue, from pier jump to beach landing. And in full-color, 1080p HD to boot.

Señor Muybridge wirelessly uploaded his video to YouTube, Instagram, and his Facebook page right from the beach. In the forty-six minutes it took Yegor to drive us home to Pasadena, the video had already been viewed two dozen times. Then a buddy of Muybridge posted the YouTube link to Reddit. From there it went to Fark, Den of Geek, and io9. By the time Val had eaten an extra-large dinner of Cheerios and three squeezy pouches, the YouTube view count had risen to a few hundred. Once she'd finished her bath (screaming the whole time), we were at 1,400. When I put her to bed at seven p.m., it had spiked to 4,500 and change. And when my parents got home at ten fifteen p.m., the total views were at 54,071. The video had been relinked at over a dozen websites, and Fletcher was texting me every two seconds.

"Superkid," as the masses had dubbed my sister, was going viral.

"Hello, hello," Brynn called as she and my dad entered the front door. They both looked a little flushed and extra-smiley. "How did it go?"

I sat up on the living room couch, hiding my phone behind my back. It had been only eight hours since they'd left me to babysit Val, but it seemed like eight years. "Fine," I said. "Easy. No big deal." My phone buzzed in my hand like an angry wasp. "How about you guys? How was the show?"

"So much fun," said my stepmom, taking off her heels. "Way more exciting than what you see on TV. Impressive stagecraft. Not too many snacks, though. I am *starving*." Brynn dropped her pile of stuff—she couldn't go anywhere without at least a big purse, a water bottle, and a travel coffee mug—and beelined for the fridge.

"You didn't have any trouble?" said my dad, placing a heavy hand on my shoulder. "I know it was a lot to ask on short notice."

I put on my most winning smile. "Actually, the time flew by. If you guys want, I can watch Val a little more from now on. Save you some money on Shelby?" I'd practiced the next bit several times to make it sound as casual as possible. "I know I've been kind of checked out since the baby was born, but I'd like to spend more time with her. After all, she's my only sister."

"Really?" Brynn stood in the kitchen doorway, a box of Trader Joe's vanilla almond granola in hand. I nodded, and she came rushing across the room to wrap me in a lung-crushing hug. "Oh, hon, we've been waiting for you to say that! I know it's hard with a new baby, and we don't want you to resent her, but if you're willing, I think it'd be wonderful. Wonderful."

"Can you loosen it up a bit?" I asked in a strangled voice.

"Of course! Sorry." She let me go, brushing at her eyes. "I'm just so happy you two finally bonded. Right, Mike?"

My dad sized me up, perplexed. "You wanna spend your summer vacation babysitting?"

"Well, maybe not all day, every day," I said grudgingly. "I do have a life, you know." My phone was now buzzing so much, it was making my butt go numb. "Maybe we can start with a few afternoons a week and see how it goes?"

"Of course, of course," said Brynn. "We don't want to smother you."

"Sounds good," I said, muffling my phone with my hand. "Well, I'm pretty tired after all that baby stuff, so . . . I'm gonna . . . go to bed."

I hurried to my room, hearing my dad and Brynn celebrate as I shut the door. It made me feel a little guilty, but technically, I hadn't lied about anything. I *had* had a great time with Val, and I definitely wanted to spend more time with her. It just wasn't in the way my parents imagined.

And besides, I had other fish to fry right now. I had ten missed calls from Fletcher and seven Google updates. I was just about to check the video's view count when my phone buzzed again. Fletcher. I pressed the accept button and made sure my door was locked.

"Go to the KTLA live stream," he said, skipping the small talk. "Local news is doing a story on us right now!"

"Seriously?" I opened a Web browser on my MacBook Air and Googled "KTLA live stream." A video window opened, showing an advertisement for hemorrhoid cream. "Ugh, who is the audience for this?" I complained.

"Old people," he informed me grimly.

Finally the newscast began to play. I chewed the skin around my fingernails as spray-tanned, shoulder-padded anchor Susannah Banks introduced our story.

"Up in the sky, it's a bird, it's a plane, it's . . . Superkid? People on the Santa Monica Pier were astonished earlier today when a man with a *baby* strapped to his chest leapt into the Pacific Ocean to save a man who had fallen off the pier. As you can see in this exclusive video, some sort of apparatus lifted the man, baby, and adult rescuer out of the water to safety. Channel Five spoke with the victim about his near-death experience."

A shot of Flannel Guy appeared on screen. His onscreen chyron read *Bodhi Morning—Rescued by "Superkid."* The cut on his forehead had been dressed with a large beige Band-Aid. He had changed out of his wet flannel shirt into a dry one, but had neglected to comb his shoulder-length stringy blond hair for his television appearance. "Oh, she was definitely for real, man," said Bodhi. "Crying, kicking those chubby little legs . . . I still don't know how I managed to fall off the pier, but whoever that baby is, I owe her my life."

The broadcast cut back to the news anchor. "Others in the Los Angeles area also want to know the identity of 'Superkid.' While local authorities have yet to file charges, they did say the mystery rescuer is, quote, 'wanted for questioning.' Police released these composite sketches of the perpetrators." Rough drawings of me in my fast-food bag and my baby sister appeared onscreen. The likenesses were pretty good. Our estimated heights, weights, and ages were listed beside them. "If you have any information, please call the number you see below. Moving on to sports, the Clippers weren't so super this evening. . . ."

I closed the live-stream window. "See that? They called you a 'man,'" said Fletcher.

"I'm also wanted for questioning!" I replied, attempting not to scream the words. "Everybody thinks I'm a *criminal*."

"Not everybody. Go look at Twitter. 'Superkid' is trending locally!"

I opened the website and clicked on the Superkid hashtag. There were hundreds pictures, comments, and retweets of Muybridge's video. I quickly scanned the first page:

WTF??? Is this for real?! #Superkid
#SUPERKID??? More like SUPER KEWL!!!!
Can we send #Superkid to N Korea???
#Superkid vid a TOTAL FAKE. Worst Photoshop EVAAAH
THE #SUPERKID VIDEO = CHILD ABUSE!!!!! #arrestthisman

I looked closer at the last comment. It had been posted by—oh crap—Fran Caulder. Fran was a conservative infotainment journalist who, according to my dad, was famous for two things: she was surprisingly attractive for a hardcore conservative, and she could drop a venomous rant on any topic, regardless of whether or not she knew the facts. She hosted a daily radio show, broadcast five hours a week on Fox News, and had written several best-selling books with titles like *Everything You Know Is Wrong* and *America Is Over*. Her comment had 1,100 favorites so far and had been retweeted 741 times.

"That knee-jerk, uniformed…lickspittle," I said. "She went straight to the nuclear option."

"You should be psyched. People wait years to get this kind of attention."

"Fletcher. She's saying I committed *child abuse*."

"She's a nutjob. Look at all the people out there who love Superkid. You're getting memed, dude! Have you seen the Superkid Obama poster?"

I scrolled down and found it—a red-and-blue hued rip-off of the iconic 2008 Obama "Hope" poster. In place of the president, though, there was a blurry screen grab of me and my sister flying through the air. Even with the poor picture quality, it looked badass. "Great, let me know when they have it in a men's medium. In the meantime, I'm flaming this troll." I clicked on the message window and began to compose a tweet. "@FranCaulder, as Superkid's brother, I can say you have no FRIGGIN' idea—"

Fletcher made the sound of squealing car tires. "Slow your roll, Quick Draw. Are you posting this as yourself?"

"Yeah. So what?" I'd been on Twitter for a couple years. It was a great way to follow comic book artists and writers. I'd posted over a thousand tweets, but I had only eighty-six followers. Maybe this Superkid business would change that.

"So, think about it. If you out yourself as Superkid's brother . . ."

The red curtain of rage before my eyes lifted slightly. "Crap."

"Exactly. I know it sucks to read all this, but if you get famous, you get trolled. Them's the rules of the Interwebs. Fran Caulder's stuff isn't even the worst out there."

"What could be worse than that?"

I heard him tapping on his laptop. "Let's see . . . You have people saying you should be arrested . . . people pushing for execution . . . This one wants you to watch childcare videos until your eyes bleed. So, you know, the usual."

"This happened six hours ago. I'm already getting *death threats?*"

"We're in a digital age. Stuff happens at the speed of thought."

"Well, we have to respond. Tell these psychos they're wrong. We'll just set up a, what do you call it? An anonymous account. A *bunch* of anonymous accounts."

"Even if you do a thousand, there are thousands of trolls out there. It's like my dad says: 'If you wanna stop bad press, you gotta get out ahead of it.' What we need to do is redirect the conversation. Show people you're a good guy." I heard him take a bite out of what was most likely a Twinkie or a MoonPie. His next words were said around a mouthful of processed sugar: "You know how I don't like Superman?"

This was an understatement. After we'd seen the latest *Man of Steel* movie on opening night, Fletcher had spent three hours railing against why the most well-known comic book hero was, from a dramatic perspective, terrible. I won't go into it here, but it involved references to classic mythology, the Bible, and even a couple of graphs. "I remember the broad strokes."

"Well, there's one thing Supes gets right. And it's the same thing that makes Batman, Spider-Man, the X-Men, and almost every other superhero out there feared and despised by the general public."

"He's an alien."

"Interesting guess, but no." He allowed for a dramatic pause, and another bite of his dessert. "Superman. Has. Great. PR."

I was not impressed. "That's just 'cause he helps people. Being selfless is his whole deal."

"Spider-Man helps people, but half the people in New York hate his guts. Why?"

"I don't know. He leaves webbing all over the place?"

"No, that stuff dissolves away in an hour. People love Superman because of *Lois Lane.*" He let that sink in. "Lois, she writes Pulitzer Prize–winning articles for the *Daily Planet* about her Kryptonian boy toy, right? Whereas Spidey is stuck with J. Jonah Jameson." Also a fictional comic book journalist, J.J. was the editor-in-chief of New York's made-up *Daily Bugle*. "He's constantly dragging Spider-Man's name through the mud, offering rewards for his capture, and so on. The difference? PR." There was a muffled *thump* as Fletcher literally dropped the mic, or in this case, his phone.

"Okay . . . so how do we get that?" I asked once he picked the phone back up.

"Good question. It's gotta be something we can control, like an article, or a podcast interview . . . something that proves Val's powers aren't the result of Photoshop or a levitation belt. Something that shows everyone her abilities don't hurt her, and all we want to do is help people."

It was a solid idea. If disgraced politicians, CEOs, and celebrities could use the media to do damage control, why not a superhero? "So how do we do that? I don't have the money to hire a publicist."

"Maybe we could email some journalists. Offer an exclusive."

"What if they make us look like monsters? Or they figure out who we are?" I chewed more skin off my fingertips. "We need to do this in a way that there's no chance of us getting caught." I clicked to refresh the Superkid video window on YouTube. 178,433 views now.

"The video," I said, snapping my fingers in realization. "That's it."

I heard Fletcher tear open another snack cake. "What's 'it'?" he asked around a mouthful of high-calorie processed sweets.

I shut my laptop. "We're gonna make an announcement video."

"Let's talk costumes."

Fletcher stood on my back patio, a large storage unit's worth of comic books, movies, and art materials spread on the picnic table between us. He had arrived at my door front at eight thirty on Monday morning, mere minutes after Brynn and my dad left for work. It was the earliest I'd gotten up all summer.

Shelby was in the kitchen feeding Val breakfast, so Fletcher and I moved to the backyard. It was fairly private, with cinder-block walls on two sides and a detached garage with a second-story studio apartment above it on the third. Not a bad spot to make top-secret plans.

And, man, did we need a plan. As of that morning, the Superkid video had 12,360,241 total views on YouTube alone. In the sixteen hours since the rescue, Val's chubby magnetic body had floated through Internet servers all over the world. The likes had risen, but the dislikes were still on top, and the haters were now calling for my blood in a dozen different languages. Hot Dog on a Stick had offered a month's free food to whoever could positively ID Superkid or her "degenerate handler." We needed to shoot our response video, and we needed to get it out there ASAP.

"Why do we need costumes?" I complained. "I can just throw another fast-food bag over my head."

"This is your reveal to the world," said Fletcher emphatically. "Your coming-out party. Your 'I am Iron Man' moment. You wanna go down as the first fast-food superhero?"

"Ugh, fine. So long as we respond quickly. And no spandex." I took a bite from one of the glazed chocolate doughnuts Fletcher had brought from Mr Goods. "Formfitting? Not the best look for me." I'd always been skinny, but I didn't particularly want my spindly chicken limbs showcased for the entire world.

"A costume is not just about looks," Fletcher said. "It's your brand, your philosophy, your whole superhero persona. Not to mention the most important part—concealing your identity."

He fanned out a stack of comics. All the big guns were there— Superman, Spider-Man, Batman, Iron Man, The X-Men—along with some smaller titles, such as Hellboy, Spawn, One-Punch Man, Lumberjanes, and Saga.

"Take a good, long look," he said. "What's the first thing you notice?"

I glanced at the comics. "Muscles."

"Come on, dude. This is important." Again, there was that weird earnestness. A serious, impassioned Fletcher was going to be difficult for me to get used to.

I sighed in annoyance, but made an effort to study the drawings. I tried to see them from a film student perspective, analyzing the images for artistic, compositional, and metaphorical value.

"Strength," I began. "Color. Low-angle shots . . . action poses . . . determination?"

"Bravery, good," he corrected me. "Why do you think we call them 'heroes'? Because they're the ones who walk toward the fight, who put themselves in harm's way, who use their powers to do what no one else can. These characters represent the ideal aspirations of all humanity. And the costume is a symbol for those ideals."

It was definitely too early for a philosophy lecture. I stuffed another doughnut in my mouth. "Cut to the chase. Which ideals do you want our costume to represent?"

"Actually, I was hoping you had some suggestions," Fletcher admitted. "Everything on Google is pretty generic Superman knockoff stuff." He held out his iPad. There were dozens of images, mostly cartoons, of kids in capes and masks.

"Boring," I agreed. "And unpractical. Most of these outfits don't even have pockets, much less a place to store baby wipes."

"Baby wipe . . . storage," he dutifully wrote on a notepad program. "What else do we need? Let's blue-sky this. Function and form, go."

"Well, the baby carrier is great for toting her around—we need that. Then there's all the cleanup stuff—extra diapers, diaper cream, spit-up cloths, change of clothes, formula bottles . . ."

"Maybe we could do, like, a utility belt for some of that?" He began sketching a mock-up, with a wipe container and bottle bandolier.

"And we'll need protection," I said. "They make all kinds of baby helmets these days. Slap a visor or something on it to protect her identity. And keep the sun out of her eyes. Helmets are a good idea for both of us, actually. Batman uses one."

He added that to the list. "Elbow and knee pads, too? Maybe some kind of chest protector? Will you be running with her?"

"I can. But I don't want to jostle her too much."

"Comfortable . . . shoes," he wrote. "You notice how every superhero ever wears boots? They're, like, skintight, too. Can you imagine the calf sweat?"

"Let's keep it simple. I already have a pair of black Doc Martens."

"Doc . . . Martens," wrote Fletcher. "What about pants? You want bike shorts? Cargos?"

"Jeans, please," I said. I had not loved the look of my dangling flamingo sticks protruding from my cargo shorts during our Santa Monica rescue. "Ooh, and gloves. The fingerless kind, like bikers wear. Just 'cause they're cool."

He jotted it down. "What about communication? GPS, email? You might want to Instagram it when you catch a bad guy."

"It'll have to be something I can easily access," I said. "Can't be digging in my pocket every time I get a tweet."

"How about an Apple Watch?"

"Too small to type on," I said. "They sell wristband holders for phones, though. That could work."

"Great. Now for the big one. Cape?"

We looked at each other, silently debating the pros and cons of that most iconic piece of superhero attire. The 2004 animated film *The Incredibles* had a great comedic scene about the detriments of capes, but they did make for a great photo op. Still . . .

"'No capes,'" we quoted in unison.

Fletcher began sketching out a wire frame figure, which I presumed would soon be me. "Any ideas for a color scheme?"

"Ugh, I suck at this stuff. I can't even tell the difference between turquoise and aquamarine." I finished off my doughnut, wiping crumbs from my shirt. "Let's just go with black. Black doesn't show dirt."

"And it's slimming," he said pointedly. I flicked doughnut crumbs at him. "What about an accent color, though? Something that matches the 'I have a baby girl strapped to my chest' persona. Is pink too on the nose?"

"Yes," I said firmly.

"Yellow? Blue? Paisley?"

"Don't care. Let's just keep it low-key."

"I'll try some things," he said. He closed his iPad and started stacking his comics. "You start thinking of what you're going to say in this video. You need a better catchphrase than 'Stay safe out there.'"

"Right." I was still embarrassed by the cheesy outro I'd given to Bodhi Morning. At least no one had caught it on camera. I'd hate to think of the comments *that* would have generated.

* * *

We reconvened Wednesday afternoon, right after Val went down for her nap and Shelby had gone home for the day. My dad and Brynn were a little surprised that I still wanted to babysit, but a couple rounds of puppy-dog eyes had convinced them to let me do a weekday trial afternoon. A video baby monitor was set up on the patio table so I could keep tabs on my napping sister. The rescue video views had now crept to over forty million. At least a dozen more websites had picked up the story. Most people seemed to think the video was fake, but everyone was still clamoring to know our identities. Several news outlets had offered to interview us over video chat, but Fletcher and I agreed we shouldn't talk to anyone until after our announcement video had debuted.

My friend unboxed the outfits we had chosen. There were black motorcycle helmets for me and Val, complete with sun visors to protect our identities and a purple and silver SK logo. There was also a black leather duster jacket, a black baby carrier, motorcycle gloves, and pre-scuffed black jeans.

"How'd you get all this stuff so quickly?" I asked, peering through the motorcycle helmet's visor.

"Amazon Prime, dude. I set up a business account and paid for everything with Bitcoin so it can't be traced back to us. Got it all with free next-day shipping to boot."

I set down the helmet and pulled on the gloves. "It looks awesome. I love the *Fast & Furious* vibe."

"Right?" he said. "Not too on the nose, but the purple hits the girl power angle. You ready to do this?"

While I went to get changed, Fletcher set up the camera, lights, and microphone in the living room. The idea was to make the background as bland as possible, so no one could identify where we lived. Val woke from her nap as I was getting ready, so I wrangled her into her costume as well. It was a simple purple onesie with black, faux leather booties. Like any child-related activity, it took much longer than expected and there were unforeseen issues. I could barely hear or see in my visored motorcycle helmet, and Val kept trying to kick her booties off. Worse, when I cinched her into the baby carrier, she strained against the straps and kicked her tiny, booted heels painfully against my hip bones.

Despite all of this, I finally got us dressed. We stepped into the living room to show Fletcher the full effect. He didn't smile or clap or even point at us and laugh. Instead he covered his mouth with one hand and turned away.

"Is it that terrible?" I asked. "It's terrible, isn't it?" I looked at our reflections in the mirror. "I knew it. I look like an underage biker in this—holy crap. Are you *crying?*"

Fletcher shook his head, too fast, but his eyes were wet. He took a steadying breath. "It's just, seeing you guys like that . . . you look like real superheroes." He tried to smile, but started to tear up again. "And I never thought I'd be part of . . . something like this."

I went over and awkwardly patted him on the shoulder. "You're part of it, okay? Now quit freaking me out."

"You're right," he said, clearing his throat. "Whew. Okay, I'm better now."

"Good, then you can tell me if anything's out of place." I twisted my body to make sure nothing snapped or pinched.

He adjusted the shoulders of my duster and pulled down my shirt to hide my belly. "Perfect," he said. "Steve Ditko himself couldn't have drawn it better." He got emotional again, then waved his hands. "I'm fine, really. Totally fine." A sob escaped his mouth.

With the costume and our feelings sorted, we got ready to shoot. But as soon as Fletcher began recording, we hit two more major snags. First, Val screeched every time I tried to speak. Second, the more I spoke, the more we all realized something—I'm terrible on camera.

"'Good morning, America,'" I began, reading the script I'd written on a yellow legal pad. "Wait, that's a TV show," I said to Fletcher. "How did we not catch that? How about . . . 'Hello.' 'How's it going?' 'Greetings.' 'Greetings, America.'" I broke character again. "Do we want to be so USA-centric, though? 'Greetings, world. Greetings, humans. Greetings, people of Earth.' Now I sound like a sci-fi robot!"

"Cut." Fletcher stood up from behind his newly-purchased Canon 7D camera. "Dude, you're freaking yourself out. Relax for a second. Shake out that tension. Go on." He demonstrated, wiggling his hands and legs. I copied him half-heartedly. Val screeched. "Now. Forget the words, take a deep breath, and speak from the heart. What do you want to tell us about your sister?"

I slowly filled my lungs, then secured the motorcycle helmet on my head. "Okay. Take two." I braced my hands on my hips and fixed my gaze on the camera. My voice dropped two octaves to a guttural Christian-Bale-gargling-gravel range. "'What's up, world. I'm Superbro.'"

"Cut," said Fletcher. "Really? A Batman voice?"

I flipped up the visor of my helmet. I'd only been wearing the thing for five minutes, and my head was already swampier than the Florida Everglades. "I thought, maybe add some gravitas to it. Show people we're serious?"

"You have a baby superhero strapped to your chest," he reminded me. "We're not remaking *The Dark Knight* trilogy. Lighten it up."

I flipped the visor back down. I swung my head back and forth to loosen the rock-hard tension in my neck. "Be myself, be myself. Okay. Ready?"

"Still rolling," he said.

Val screeched again, so I instinctively bounced up and down to soothe her. "Okay. Hi, everybody. Superkid's brother here. A lot of people have been talking about me and my sister the last few days, saying I'm a bad sibling, and I feel like the time has come for me to respond."

Fletcher gave me a thumbs-up, gesturing for me to keep going. I took a breath. "First off, apologies for the getup, but with all the trolling we've received, including some full-on threats—*cough* Fran Caulder *cough*—I feel the need to protect our identities. Second, my sister's powers are real. And despite the hundreds of comments to the contrary, they do not hurt her." Val babbled as I started to loosen the straps on the baby carrier. "Ready?"

Fletcher zoomed out to a wide shot, giving me a nod. I lifted Val out of the baby carrier, holding her straight in front of me. Thankfully, she was tolerating her helmet for the moment.

"Observe," I said, and dropped my baby sister on the hardwood floor.

Val dropped toward the hard surface, then ricocheted back up with a peppy, cartoon *boing*. I let her bounce once, twice, three times, then reached out to catch her, but her EM field made her repel away from my hands. She shot across the room, pinged off the dining room table, bumped the hanging microphone, and somersaulted toward Fletcher's camera. She squealed delightedly as she kicked off the tripod, knocking it back two feet. Her chubby body spun back in a perfect arc toward my face. Animal instinct made me block my face, and she landed gently in my arms. Her EM field went back to normal.

Val cooed, clapping her hands together softly. "See?" I said to the camera with barely contained relief. "She loves it."

Val gave a singsongy velociraptor shriek of confirmation. I settled her back inside the baby carrier. "And to all those people who think I'm mistreating my kid sis by doing this—what she can do is a miracle. It would be selfish not to use it to help people."

Sufficiently relaxed now, I segued back into our prewritten speech. "So. Anyone with serious requests for assistance can send them to superkid, all one word, at iamsuperkid.com. Superkid.com was taken. Thanks, organic baby food company." Fletcher and I had spent the last few days setting up Superkid's social media presence, which besides the website included accounts on Twitter, Facebook, Instagram, and LinkedIn.

I cleared my throat before continuing. "Jobs we will not consider: anything life-threatening, anything more than a four-hour drive from Southern California, military action, espionage, public appearances, and any other kind of activity we deem harmful or uncool. Thank you for your kind attention, and bad guys beware"—here I pointed a gloved finger at the camera—"there's a new kid on the playground."

"And . . . cut." Fletcher stopped recording and stood up from the camera, a big goofy grin on his face. "That's the one, man. Let's see how the people of Earth respond to that."

The Superkid announcement video went live on YouTube at 1:22 p.m. on June 12. In the first twenty-four hours, it was viewed 14 million times, retweeted 3,456 times, and favorited by 10,641 people. Eighty-seven thousand people clicked to follow @officialsuperkid on Twitter, and 231,000 liked our Facebook fan page. Public opinion, however, was still very much up in the air. We had our fans, but Fletcher's fears had been proven right—most people still thought Val's powers were done with special effects. Even more flocked to the Fran Caulder camp, saying it didn't matter if my baby sister appeared unhurt—I'd purposefully dropped her on the floor, and that was abuse.

Despite those accusations (or maybe because of them), the Superkid website had 13,500 unique views in the first day. The volume of traffic crashed our host server twice. We received nearly a hundred emails. About half of them were requests for interviews or more information, while another few dozen alternated between messages of support and screeds of condemnation. The remaining twenty-five or so were legitimate appeals for help. Shelby was watching Val that day, so I went over to Fletcher's to hang out by his pool as we went through emails.

The Grossman house was a Spanish-style mansion tucked into the foothills of Altadena, with a ten-foot privacy wall surrounding it on three sides. Bougainvillea hung from the redwood pergola slats above us. A waterfall splashed gently into the pool behind us. Fletcher's cook Ximena had left us a tray of cookies and lemonade. I loved coming here.

"'Dear Superkid,'" Fletcher read off his iPad, "'I am a six-year-old boy living in Redlands, California.' Awww."

"That's only sixty minutes away," I said, already excited.

"'I think your powers are so cool. Please can you teach me how to make myself bounce off the walls and floor like you do? I have tried, but only given myself bruises. My mom says I need to stop because I'll hurt myself, but if you can do it, then I can too, right? Please help, I want to be a superhero like you. Your friend, Ronan.'"

"Poor kid," I said. "We should have added a 'do not try this at home' disclaimer to the announcement video."

"Already on it," said Fletcher, editing our video description text on YouTube. "Last thing we need is a lawsuit."

"What could they sue us for? It's not like we told people to imitate Val."

"This is America, dude. My dad says people can sue anyone for *anything*." He quickly scanned the new disclaimer text, then saved the changes. "Your turn."

I bent over my laptop. "This one's from Akiko Miyamoto in Santa Barbara. 'Dear Superkid. Congratulations on your YouTube success. It is nice to see people respond to something so miraculous and positive. I'm hoping that, if your powers exist, there can be other kinds of miracles in the world as well. My mother has . . .' Oh man." I swallowed, then continued in a less upbeat voice. "'My mother has stage four stomach cancer. We have tried everything, but she is now in hospice, and she is not expected to live through the week. Does your power work on other people? Perhaps you could repel my mother's cancer, the way you repel your own body. I am sorry to put you on the spot like this, but I am desperate. Thank you very much for your consideration, and may God bless you.'" I sat back from the laptop. "Well, that's super, all right. Super-depressing."

Fletcher shrugged his broad shoulders. "It sucks, but who does she think we are—Dr. Superkid, MD? Even if Val could pass on her powers, does she think we have the time to go around, magnetizing the boo-boos of every person in a two-hundred-and-fifty-mile radius? It would take years."

Even for Fletcher, this was harsh. "Dude, her mom's dying. She's grasping at straws."

"Yeah, well, everyone's got something. You do what the rest of us do—suck it up, move on, and quit wasting other people's time with nonsense." He tapped his iPad. "Now, here's one with some actual hero factor. 'Dear Superkid. I don't know if ur real"—he read *ur* like it was spelled—"or if ur some kind of Internet stunt, but I need help. I'm fourteen years old, and I live in Lancaster, California. My dad beats me up." His face flushed, but he continued reading. "My mom doesn't do anything to stop him. She tells me I need to toughen up. Can you please help me? Sincerely, Tim.' And there's an address." He set down his iPad and looked at me expectantly.

"What do you want us to do?" I said. "Walk into this kid's house and punch his dad in the face? 'Cause that's not heroism, that's assault."

Fletcher's face turned the color of bruised grape. "So is what this dad is doing. And to his own son, Robbie! This kid is asking us—he's begging us—to stop it."

I knew Fletcher's relationship with his own father was strained. Rath (he pronounced it "Wraith") Grossman was a man's man, who prided himself on his physical strength, his successful career, and his own ego. To say Fletcher was not what he expected in a son was an understatement. My friend had even told me that he thought his dad scheduled extra business trips so he wouldn't have to hang out with him. When he was in town, Mr. Grossman's steady stream of pep talks, critiques, and straight-up insults made Fletcher wish he'd stay away permanently. He was an intimidating man to be around, but I had never suspected their bad blood was due to something like this.

I squirmed uncomfortably. "I just don't think, in this particular case, more violence is the answer. Why don't we call the cops? Leave an anonymous tip. We have Tim's address. We'll tell them what's happening and let them handle it."

Fletcher got up, pacing back and forth on the patio. "Because that never works," he said. "They come, there's a hearing, everyone plays nice, and in six months it's back to business as usual. This dad needs to be put in his—"

He stopped as a figure exited the downstairs office and began crossing the pool patio. It was Rath himself. He was a short, mostly bald man with a close-cropped band of dark orange hair encircling his head. A wine-colored sweater and tan slacks showed off his powerful build. He was in the middle of a phone call but came to a halt when he saw us.

"What'd I tell you about the cookies, Fletcher?" he asked, his voice soft but steel-tipped.

My best friend reddened, stepping to block Mr. Grossman's view of the plate. "I only had one, Dad."

"He did," I said quickly. "He's been really good about monitoring his—"

"It's Robbie, isn't it?" Mr. Grossman asked. His pale gray eyes flicked toward me. His intense, unblinking stare made me want to hide under the table. "Robbie, please don't interrupt when I'm talking to my son." His eyes went back to Fletcher.

"I'll . . . I'll take them inside," Fletcher said miserably. He turned and picked up the plate.

"Good," said his father. "Because a man who can't control himself won't control anything else." He went back to his phone call, striding into the main house.

Fletcher took the plate of cookies into the kitchen. When he returned, the resentment he'd been feeling seemed to have faded. "Where were we?" he asked.

"Um . . . we were talking about how to use Val's powers. I thought we should be focused more on getting cats out of trees and catching shoplifters."

"Right, right. You're right, we shouldn't do anything violent right off the bat, I guess." The fire he'd had before was completely gone from his voice.

We awkwardly read a few more emails, but thankfully the chimes of Fletcher's expensive doorbell interrupted us. Ximena stuck her head out of the patio door. She was a pleasant Latina woman in her mid-forties with braided black hair and kind eyes. Behind her stood Patty Nakong, radiating fury from every cell of her tiny frame.

"You have a guest, Señor Grossman," said Ximena. "Would you like more lemonades?"

"Sure, Ximena. But small glasses, please. We're controlling our calories." The housekeeper inclined her head, shutting the patio door.

"You. Two-faced. *Dingleberries*," Patty whispered fiercely.

"Patty Cakes," said Fletcher, going over to give her a hug. She shoved him away. "I've been meaning to return your texts, and here you are."

She angrily jabbed her enormous glasses higher on her button nose. "You two bring me the biggest genetic discovery since natural selection, tell me to keep it a frakking secret, then you go out and make a *YouTube video?*"

"We had to," Fletcher explained, holding out his hands as if she were a wild animal. "After that first one went viral—which was totally not our doing, by the way—we had to respond somehow. What we were supposed to do, let Robbie get arrested?"

"People have made bigger sacrifices in the service of science," she growled. "In fact, it's two of the basic tenets—keep your work secret, and DO NOT go public until you can prove your discovery!"

"But we did prove it," he said soothingly.

"You don't know why she floated! Maybe it was on purpose, maybe it was an accident. Maybe that's just her version of breaking wind!"

"Nah, her farts are stinkier," I said. "I can vouch for that."

Fletcher bit back a smile, but Patty folded her arms. "You guys got lucky. The only thing your 'announcement video' proves is that you're not ready for this. You couldn't even bounce Valeria without sending her all over the room like a piece of Flubber. You need to do tests, take measurements, develop safety guidelines . . ."

Fletcher took her by the shoulders. All the tension coiled in his body during our argument seemed to have disappeared. "Which is why we need you on the team," he said soothingly. "Help us categorize and collate and what have you. Be the Watson to our Sherlock."

Patty shrugged him off. "First of all, if anything, you two are the Watsons to *my* Sherlock." Fletcher rolled his eyes. "Second, this whole enterprise needs a very large helping of the scientific method." She took out her iPhone, opened an app, and began speaking into it. "Audio Log One, Superkid Testing Trials. Now, Robbie, when the subject floated, did you notice any particular feelings?"

"You're recording this?" I asked.

"You want me on board, I'll be recording everything from here on out. Did you feel anything?"

"You mean, other than excruciating pain? At the time, I was floating fifty feet above the ocean with an unconscious man dangling from my hip."

"You didn't feel any vibrations? Electric currents? Anything like that?"

"No, but there was this kind of low-pitched hum," I remembered. "You think that has something to do with her EM field?"

"No idea," she said happily. "Would you be willing to attempt another trial?"

Fletcher and I were more than eager to set aside our argument over what Superkid's first official act of heroism should be in favor of testing Val's superpowers. By the time Ximena brought out our lemonade refills, the three of us had made up a comprehensive list of ways to determine my baby sister's strengths and weaknesses.

The next step, however, was to put them into practice.

Over the next two weeks, Fletcher, Patty, and I went into full-on Jedi training mode. Our first goal was to determine what circumstances triggered Val's repelling instinct. We knew that startling her worked, but I couldn't carry a hundred bags of chips on my body. We had to find other, more controllable ways to activate her powers.

First we strapped Val to my chest and I let myself fall forward. The baby gave a grunt of surprise, but did not increase her EM field. I had to throw out my arms to catch us both. We then tried hopping off the front porch, the dining room table, and the hood of Mr. Grossman's GMC Sierra pickup. The only result was a bit of fussing from my jostled sister.

Loud noises were more successful. We first tried clapping and yelling, but the most Val did was knock me back a foot or two. We moved up to noisemakers, using phone alarms and handheld buzzers before finally deciding to try an air horn.

Fletcher recorded the test on his Canon 7D and Patty readied a stopwatch while I stepped in front of the camera. "This is Superkid,

EM Test Number Sixty-Seven," I said. "We are now going to see the effects of an air horn."

I pressed the device. The blaring, atonal sound made Val's eyes go wide. There was a familiar *boing*, and both she and I launched forty feet into the air. I was so startled, I dropped the air horn. I looked down at the roof of my house, seeing a plastic Wiffle ball in one of the gutters. I'd been wondering where that had gone. We dropped back down, only it wasn't the gradual descent we'd experienced at the pier. Val and I fell like a hundred-pound boulder.

"Magnetize!" I told her. "Repel! Float! You better do something, or—"

BLAAAT! Two feet from the ground, Fletcher hit the air horn again.

Val's EM field increased, and we went another ten feet into the air. This time the drop back down was short enough that I was able to absorb the landing with my legs.

"Well, that works," said Fletcher.

"I think . . . we need some more practice . . . before we take that one into the field," I said, panting.

Patty came forward, tallying up some numbers. "Actually, we now have several proven methods for activating her EM response. I think we're ready to—"

BEEP BEEP. A car horn blooped from the front of the house. It sounded like Brynn's Prius alarm. Actually, it sounded *exactly* like Brynn's Prius alarm. I checked the iPhone attached to my left wrist: 5:45 p.m.? My stepmom was home from work early.

"Hide everything!" I whisper-yelled to Fletcher and Patty. I jogged across the patio, trying to pull off my Superkid duster jacket. I'd put on Val's baby carrier on over the leather, so it was now sandwiched to my body in various places. One sleeve flapped free as I ran over to my co-conspirators. They merely stared at me.

"So, am I cutting here, or . . .?" said Fletcher.

"Cut!" I said, pressing the button on the camera. "My stepmom's home."

"Oh," he said. Then: *"Oh."*

To his credit, he immediately began to break down the camera equipment as if he were fieldstripping a rifle while at the business end of another rifle.

Patty, however, merely arched an eyebrow. "You haven't told your *parents* we're doing this? I believe I speak for women, mothers, and childcare providers everywhere when I say—"

"Say it later!" I hissed at her. "Now hide your data!"

"Just so you know, I am a terrible liar!" she hissed back. "Like, world-class, across-the-board *bad.*" But she began to gather her scattered notes into a pile.

I unhooked Val's helmet and tossed it in her jungle seat. I pulled my sister out of the baby carrier, placing her on a blanket in the grass. While she babbled at the sky, I attempted to unhook the baby carrier straps from my torso. Then I realized Val was still in her Superkid onesie. I had no idea if Brynn had seen the announcement video yet (I certainly hadn't sent her a link), but I couldn't risk her recognizing it. I trotted over to my baby sister, shucking off my leather coat along the way. The carrier flapped around my legs. I bent over the baby, unsnapping the shirt at her crotch and pulling it over her chubby tummy and arms. I looked for a place to stash the incriminating outfit, finally deciding to jam it in the pocket of my jeans. I had just stuffed the last purple corner of it down my pants when Brynn slid open the back patio door.

"Hey, guys," she said, curiously taking in Fletcher, who was nonchalantly draping his coat over the camera case, and Patty, who stood as still as a totem pole.

"Hello!" I shouted in an oddly singsong voice. *Act normal, dummy.*

"I mean, hi. You're home early." I jogged over to awkwardly hug my stepmom. The baby carrier straps clacked the whole way.

"I finished my depos early and thought I'd give you a break. What's with the motorcycle helmet?" She indicated my headgear. "And why is Val naked?"

Crud. I unstrapped the helmet, pulling it off my sweaty head. "Good question. We were just, uh . . ." I had nothing. I looked to Fletcher for help.

"Actually, it's kind of funny," he said. "Robbie, Mouse—I mean, Patty and I were, ah . . . doing something. With Val. And we had to take her shirt off." He turned to Patty. "Right?"

The tiny girl swallowed as if she were facing a firing squad. "Hello."

Brynn picked up Val, gave her a kiss, then tucked her against her right hip. "Okay, what's going on?"

I made a *psh* sound of disbelief. "What? Nothing."

"I'm a lawyer, honey. I can smell lies like a bloodhound. Spill it."

"We were just . . . playing?" Even to my ears, it sounded lame.

Brynn scanned the backyard, her eyes narrowed. "Something's going on." She toed over my leather jacket, revealing the purple and silver SK logo.

"Robbie said you've been super busy at work, Mrs. Cooper-Rampino," said Fletcher. "Have you been on the Internet much in the last few weeks?"

I glared pointedly at him, slashing my fingers across my throat. He raised his own hands in a calming gesture. Patty continued to do nothing. In fact, she didn't even seem to be breathing.

Brynn made her way to the jungle seat. She lifted out Val's baby helmet, tapping the SK logo with her fingertip.

Fletcher continued to extend his own finger toward the Nuclear Option button. "'Cause there's this fun video? That's been making the rounds? And I think, as a mother, you in particular would appreciate it."

"Actually, I think they took it down," I said menacingly.

"No, it went back up," he countered. "Because it wasn't as bad as *some people* thought."

"But some people," I reminded him, "thought it was much, much, *much worse.*"

I looked to Patty for help. "Hello," she said.

"Enough," said Brynn. "I get it."

"You . . . do?" I said.

"I mean, it's not exactly a spotless crime scene here. You've got the superhero costumes, the camera, all those comics—" She nodded to a massive pile we had completely overlooked. "I can see what you guys are up to."

"I'm sorry," I said quickly. "I know, I should have told you when it first started, but then it took on a life of its own, and then—"

"I told you, I get it. I think it's sweet you wanted to keep this a secret."

"It's not like we planned to keep it secret forever," I began, then the impact of what she'd said landed. "Sweet?"

Brynn put a hand on my shoulder, smiling. "Of course it is, hon. I mean, making a whole Web series—that's a big undertaking."

Fletcher and I froze. Patty, you remember, had already been that way for five minutes. "Web series?" I said cautiously.

Brynn waved a hand. "Sorry, TikToks or whatever you kids call them these days. I think it's great you're making something with your sister." She squeezed my arm. "I know the last nine months have been hard on you. A new baby, you're no longer the only child, and both me and your dad have been working so much . . . To be honest, I'm relieved. I thought you hated me for having her."

TELL HER, Patty silently mouthed to me from behind Brynn's shoulder. *Tell her the TRUTH, NOW!*

Instead I nodded wisely. "You're right," I said to Brynn. "Things have been kind of rough since she showed up. But this has been good for us." Behind my stepmom, Patty threw her hands up in disgust.

"Well, good. That's good. Anytime you need her for a shoot or whatever, you let me know. I'm gonna go feed her now, but you kids have fun." She kissed me on the cheek, started back to the house, then stopped. "Just promise me, whatever you do, it won't be like that horrible floating baby video from a couple weeks ago."

My smile collapsed like Sauron's tower at the end of *The Lord of the Rings*. "Which what now?"

"The pier rescue thing down in Santa Monica," she said. Fletcher and Patty looked at each other like a couple of raccoons caught going through the garbage. "You must have seen it; it was all over the Internet."

"You said a floating . . . baby?" said Fletcher as if he'd never heard the word before.

"Yeah, some dingbat jumped off the pier with a real baby strapped to his chest. They fell, like, fifty feet."

Now was not the time to tell her it was closer to ninety. "Oh yeahhhh," I said. "I think I heard something about it on the news. Sounds like whoever it was, they saved a guy from drowning."

"Yeah, by putting an innocent child's life in danger! The worst part is, he was wearing a bag on his head so nobody was able to identify him." She nuzzled her daughter's head. "The coward knows if people saw his face, he'd be going straight to prison."

Patty nodded vehemently. I stepped in front of her. "Could he really go to jail, though? I mean, what would they charge him with? Hypothetically."

Brynn ticked off the counts on her fingers. "Reckless endangerment of a minor. Vigilantism. Disturbing the peace. Child abuse. Did you know that child abuse victims are sixty percent more likely to be criminals when they grow up?"

My head was swimming. "Wait a minute. You think this guy's a *child abuser*?"

"Absolutely. He's, like, ten times worse than those beauty pageant moms. And he's clearly doing it for the publicity. They said the video already has 20 million views on YouTube."

Fletcher cleared his throat. "Actually, I think it's more like sixty—" His mouth closed as I elbowed him.

Brynn was in full trial lawyer mode now. "And what about the baby's rights? It's not like she decided to endanger her life to rescue that person. Her guardian forced her to do it. So yeah, I hope they ID this guy and lock him up for the rest of his life."

I tried to do a quick count of how many people on the pier might have taken a picture of me without the Hot Dog on a Stick bag on my head. I gave up when I hit all of them. "At least the baby's powers were kind of cool, right?"

But she rolled her eyes. "Magnetism? Pretty basic superpower, if you ask me. I'm sure you three will come up with something much more creative. Have fun!"

She gave us a chipper wave, then took Val inside. I fell into a patio chair, wishing it would carry me all the way to the molten center of the earth and put me out of my misery.

Fletcher plopped down beside me. "Look on the bright side, buddy. At least now you know what she thinks of all this."

"Also, everything she said is true," said Patty. "How long do you intend to keep this a secret?"

"Until I can change her mind about what we're doing, obviously," I said.

"I know one way we can do that," said Fletcher, turning his phone toward us. Onscreen, the live feed from a local news channel played. A banner at the bottom read *Hostage Taker Demands to See Superkid*. Fletcher grinned. "I think it's time we fought some crime."

Patty and I crowded around Fletcher's phone. The footage playing on his screen was from a news helicopter. Two people stood on the eighth-floor windowsill of an old loft-style apartment building in downtown LA. It was a ten-story crumbling brick pile, with a painted advertisement for something called Rexall Orderlies flaking away on the side. The kind of place that used to be a turn-of-the-century sweatshop, but was now filled with upscale apartments for rich, unshaven hipsters.

The people on the windowsill were difficult to make out, but the guy looked to be in his thirties, bald and muscular, with a heavily tattooed arm wrapped around the wrist of a woman in her late twenties. She was wearing a tank top, workout pants, and a facial expression of absolute terror. But I can't say I blamed her, since her bare feet were dangling above the street. The bald guy held her as if she weighed no more than a loaf of bread. He was shouting something, but the news camera was too far away to pick it up. I turned up the volume on Fletcher's phone to better hear the spray-tanned anchorman.

"If you're just joining us, a dramatic hostage situation is currently underway in downtown Los Angeles," the living Ken doll said in his best Anderson Cooper impression. "The unidentified man you see onscreen is threatening to drop—yes, I'm getting confirmation of this now—he says he will drop the woman to the street, unless he can talk to Superkid."

"Holy crap," Fletcher and I said in very different tones.

"This is what we've been waiting for!" my best friend continued. "We're getting called out on live TV. We gotta go help."

"Just a minute," I said, glancing inside the house. Brynn was currently feeding Val with a bottle of formula. "Are we sure he means us?"

It was a weak stall, but now that we were finally being called into action, I found myself hesitating. Fletcher cranked the newscast volume even more.

"I'm getting another report," said the anchor. "Yes, I'm hearing the man is now saying he wants to speak with the same Superkid who rescued the man at Santa Monica two weeks ago." As the newscaster continued talking, Fletcher muted the video and folded his arms. He didn't bother to offer any verbal arguments; he simply let me debate myself. It was a short exchange.

"All right," I said, fully aware of how clichéd I was about to sound. "Let's roll."

Fletcher whooped in excitement. While he and Patty started carrying supplies out to his car, I went inside the house. Brynn was in the process of burping my baby sister.

"Hey," I said. "I know you got home early, but we were gonna take Val to the park before dinner. Is it okay if we still do that? It's kind of her favorite."

Val squealed and held out her hands to me. "Oh," said Brynn in surprise. "You sure? I mean, I don't mind watching her so you can hang out with her friends."

"Right. The thing is . . ." What had she said? *Anytime you need her, let me know.* "We need to grab some more shots for the Web series. Is it okay?"

Brynn considered that, then shrugged. "Sure, honey, thanks. I was hoping to get a little gardening time in anyway."

She passed over the baby. I carried her out back to collect our superhero gear. "If at any point you're not into this," I whispered as I pulled on her onesie, "you just cry or wave your hands or something, okay?"

"Gooshee wawa," Val said.

I took that as an agreement and walked around to the front of our house. Fletcher and Patty were nearly done loading our gear into his dad's Bentley Mulsanne. It was a sleek black-and-silver personal limousine with thick tires, dark tinted glass, satellite radio, voice-control steering, and top-of-the-line everything. I Googled it once, and was stunned to see the car's base price was $303,000. This one was probably 100K more, as the rear of the vehicle had heated leather seats for six, HD satellite TV, and a high-end refrigerated bar. Yegor sat behind the wheel, his powerful frame barely contained by a trim gray suit. He was as expressionless as always.

The rear doors of the Bentley opened saloon-style, which made loading Val's car seat slightly easier. Not *easy*, mind you, since my sister absolutely despised riding in the car. My parents and I couldn't figure out if she had motion sickness or she simply hated being restrained. But anytime we went somewhere in a vehicle, Val screamed as if we were branding her with red-hot coat hangers.

Today she began to fuss as soon as I neared Fletcher's car. "I know, honey," I said as I opened the passenger door with my left hand. Taking care of a baby makes you learn how to do a lot of things as a lefty. "We're just gonna go for a little ride, then you're gonna save a woman's life, okay?"

"Unnhh, unnhhhh," said Val, screwing up her face. She pushed back from the car with her feet, beginning to slip out of my hand. I tried to readjust my grip, but there was a deep *thrum*, and Val suddenly stuck to the metal car door like a paper clip on a magnet.

"Okay, that's a new one," I said. I looked toward Yegor, but he was facing forward, his emotionless blue eyes hidden under sunglasses. "Come on, honey, no powers right now." I tried to pull her off the door, but it was like she'd been stuck there with superglue.

Fletcher approached with the last of his camera gear. "Is she using a new power? Sweet!"

"Help me with her." We both grabbed the handle of my sister's torso and yanked, but it would have been easier pulling our shadows off the ground. Val giggled, clearly under the impression that this was a game, and she was winning. "You think that's funny, young lady?" I panted, giving a series of tugs on her body. "We—are getting—in this car. Now!"

But still, she didn't budge. "What about a crowbar?" suggested Fletcher.

"I have a better idea," I said. "Time to bust out the nuclear option." I took a step toward my baby sister, my hands looming over her—

Then I tickled her squishy little armpits. "Tickle, tickle, tickle," I said in a dumb high-pitched voice. Val squealed, shaking her head in delight.

THRUM! There was another low, vibrate-y sound, and the nine-month-old popped off the door. Quickly, I placed her in the car seat and attached the straps. Realizing she'd been tricked, Val's lower lip puffed out. Her eyes glistened. Cue heartbreak in three . . . two . . . waterworks.

Big, fat baby tears rolled down my sister's adorably chubby cheeks as I dispassionately tightened the straps. She fought, but I made sure they were good and tight. If her sobs were any indication, I was

Mussolini, Hitler, and the people responsible for the *Fantastic Four* movies, all rolled into one. I slid in next to her, jamming a pacifier in her mouth. It did nothing to stop her wailing.

"What's wrong?" said Patty, dropping a load of science-y stuff on the back seat. "Is it gas? Colic? Magnetic degradation on a cellular level?"

"Nope, she just hates riding in the car," I said.

"Cloaking devices engaged," said Fletcher, entering the other side. By this, he meant he'd covered the license plates and VIN number so we couldn't be identified. Of course, if someone managed to get ahold of the Bentley and dust for fingerprints, we'd be arrested faster than you could say *CSI*.

Fletcher pressed the intercom button that enabled Yegor to hear us. "Downtown, please. Fifth and Grand." The big Russian grunted, then put the car into gear and backed down the driveway.

Patty leaned away from Val, who was still wailing at top volume. "Out of curiosity, does she cry like this the whole time she's in the car?"

"Usually!" I shouted.

"Doesn't mean we can't enjoy this!" yelled Fletcher. "How 'bout some mood music to soothe the savage beast?"

He plugged in his iPhone and selected a playlist. A thunderous, driving orchestral score filled the back seat of the Bentley. I suddenly felt like I was locked in the bedroom of a teenage Norse god who hated his father.

"What is this?" I shouted over the *BLAAAT* of electronic drums committing suicide.

"Hans Zimmer!" Fletcher yelled back. "I made a superhero compilation mix!"

Zimmer had composed the scores for almost every modern superhero film, including *The Amazing Spider-Man 2, Justice League,*

Batman v Superman, Nolan's *Dark Knight* trilogy, and *Kung Fu Panda*. His specialty was loud, bombastic stings that could knock the fillings from your teeth. On the bright side, the epic track seemed to startle Val into silence. She glanced around as if expecting to spot a herd of elephants attacking the car with metal clubs. Seeing no pachyderms, she began to fuss again. I had to hand it to the kid—she was nothing if not persistent.

"I'm not sure this is working!" I shouted.

"It's my favorite too!" Fletcher yelled back.

Three minutes later we were listening to Raffi and sitting in parking lot traffic on the 110 southbound freeway. The sweet, simple sounds of the Canadian children's troubadour had finally calmed Val down.

"We're goin' to the zoo, zoo, zoo," sang the bearded baby whisperer. *"How about you, you, you? You can come too, too, too."*

Fletcher fumed. "I want you to know, you are ruining my first superhero experience."

"Well, we'd be there by now if Yegor had taken surface streets like I suggested," I replied.

"It's rush hour; it's bad everywhere."

"Look at all the crocodiles swimmin' in the water," sang Raffi. *"Swimmin' in the water, swimming in the water."*

"At least his lyrics aren't repetitive," Patty said brightly.

It took the rest of the Raffi album and part of *The Muppet Movie* soundtrack to drive the 3.5 remaining miles to downtown LA. Yegor turned on to Fifth Street, where we saw two fire trucks, four police cars, and a half dozen news vans parked in front of the Rexall Orderlies building. Sawhorses blocked off car passage, but a crowd had gathered on the sidewalks, pointing their phone cameras upward from behind police barricades.

Fletcher pressed the intercom button. "Pull into the side alley up here, Yegor. We're, uh, just gonna hop out and get some background b-roll shots with the baby."

"You really think he's gonna buy that?" I whispered once he released the button.

Fletcher snorted. "We could blow up a cow in front of that guy and he wouldn't care."

I looked up at the Rexall building. The bald guy was still dangling his hostage over the street, one beefy hand cinched around the poor woman's wrist. A hostage negotiator was talking to him through a megaphone from the adjacent apartment window, but it looked like the cops hadn't breached yet. Two police snipers were in position on rooftops across the street.

Yegor put the Bentley in park, but kept it running. "Your communicator," Fletcher said, passing me a small earwig-style device.

I hooked it around my ear, pulled on my fingerless leather gloves, then strapped on my motorcycle helmet.

"Moment of truth," I said, trying to force more confidence into my voice than I had. "How do I look?"

"Badass. Like Judge Dredd minus the shoulder pads." While the comparison was cool, it did not settle the wriggling earthworms in my belly.

I got out of the car, unbuckling Val from her car seat. The sounds of Raffi had brought back her sweet disposition, and she gave me a dimpled smile. Patty opened her laptop, turning on a Wi-Fi travel router.

"Ready, baby girl?" I said to my sister, fitting on her protective helmet. Fletcher snapped a few pictures with his phone.

"What are you doing?" I said.

"Preserving the moment," he replied. "Trust me, you're gonna want these later."

"Well, take your time," I said sarcastically. "It's not like a woman's life depends on us or anything."

"Okay, okay." He pocketed his phone and helped me cinch Val into the baby carrier.

"Are we forgetting anything?" I asked Fletcher and Patty. "Chip bags, air horn, headset, iPhone . . ."

He handed me a compact pair of field binoculars. "We'll feed you information from here. Go get 'em, superhero."

I jogged out of the alley, Val's helmet bouncing against my chest. Fletcher had always told me that first impressions were important, so I tried to adopt Chris Evans's Captain America running style as I crossed the street. A few onlookers pointed their cameras at me as I passed. I gave them a jaunty two-finger salute.

I reached the front door of the Rexall apartment building, puffing slightly. Jogging in leather clothes with an eighteen-pound kid strapped to my chest was more tiring than I had predicted. I made a resolution to start doing more cardio tomorrow. I reached for the doorknob—

And a young police officer in dress blues stepped in front of me. "Can I help you?" he asked around a mouthful of chewing gum.

I cleared my throat, using my deepest superhero voice. "Yes. Good afternoon, officer. I'm . . . We're here to rescue the hostage."

He looked me up and down, and not in a way that made me feel like I was walking the red carpet at the Oscars. "And you are?"

"Well, she's Superkid, and I'm, uh . . ." Crap. It had been two weeks since our announcement video, and we still hadn't come up with a name for me. "I'm . . . Superkid's handler. From the YouTube videos?"

"Building's closed to lookie-loos," he said. "We got police activity upstairs."

"I know, that's why we're here," I said. "We're who the hostage taker is asking for."

"Yeah, well, I didn't hear nothing about that, kid. You can go wait with the others behind the police barricades."

I followed the line of his finger. At the front of the crowd of onlookers were three guys in Superkid knockoff costumes. Two had fast-food bags over their heads, and one had managed a pretty good approximation of my announcement video garb. All three of them had fake babies strapped to their chests.

"We already have cosplayers?" Fletcher crowed over my earpiece. "This just gets cooler and cooler!"

"We're not with them," I told the cop. "We're the real deal."

"Young man, I'm not gonna ask you again. Go back behind the barricades."

"Officer," I told him, "you are impeding justice. Now please stand aside, or I'll be forced to remove you."

The officer tilted down his mirrored sunglasses, looking me right in the eye. I put my hands on my hips, forcing myself to meet his gaze.

Less than two minutes later, though, I was back at the Bentley, my face burning with embarrassment under my helmet.

"What are you doing?" asked Fletcher. "Why'd you come back?"

"You heard what he said," I told him. "He . . . he called me a loser. Said I was interfering with the work of the real heroes." I unhooked my helmet strap. "This was dumb. Let's just go home."

Fletcher's face turned blotchy. "Screw that guy! If the cops and firefighters are doing such a great job, how come that woman's still dangling over the street? You and Val, you can't just give up! *That* would make you a loser. You've gotta get up there, now."

"They've got the whole building locked down," I said.

"They're on the eighth floor, right? Patty?" The tiny girl blinked, unsure of what he wanted from her. He mimed typing at a keyboard, and she pulled up Google Street View of our location on her laptop. Fletcher pointed to the Rexall Orderlies building, then dragged his finger to the eight-story building across the street. "If you can get to the roof of this guy, you can use Val to float across. Right, puppy?" He tickled her under the chin and she giggled.

"You know she still doesn't float on command," I reminded him.

"She will. But you guys better hurry. Baldy looks ready to drop that lady."

I sighed, but reattached my helmet to my sweaty head. "If we get arrested, it's on you."

I had no problem entering the building across the street. The doorman was on the sidewalk, rubbernecking at the hostage situation along with everyone else. He didn't even glance at my costume as I walked past.

I pushed the up button for the elevator. Suddenly Fletcher spoke into my ear. "Bad news, the cops just tried to breach. Now Baldy's yelling at them." Even in the lobby, I could hear the fearful, excited chatter of the bystanders. "You better get topside, pronto."

"Ugh." I found a door marked STAIRS and kicked it open. The stairwell stretched up above me like one of those endless M. C. Escher paintings. "It's like the frigging TARDIS in here," I complained. "Bigger on the inside." Unfortunately, since Doctor Who was not at hand, there was nothing for me to do but start jogging. Looks like I'd be getting in that extra cardio sooner than expected.

Sixteen flights of stairs and a near heart attack later, I made it to the top floor. I was drenched in sweat and wheezing. My lungs were filled with acid and my legs felt like they were coated in lava. "Siri," I wheezed into my wrist-mounted iPhone, "schedule jogging five days a week."

"I'm emailing 'thigh wages freak,'" the lady robot responded. *"Is that correct?"*

I groaned. Clearly, our AV equipment package was not yet up to Batman standards. I looked around for roof access, seeing a ladder that went up to a metal door.

"Dude, where are you?" Fletcher said over my earpiece. "The bald guy's yelling something about Fortis now. He wants a big chunk of it. And he's swinging the hostage around like a Raggedy Ann doll."

"Nearly there, "I said, climbing the ladder. "What's Fortis?"

I could hear Patty tapping it into Google. "Uh . . . probably not an investment company based out of Nova Scotia," she said. "Hold on."

I pulled back the latch on the roof door and shoved it open. Val blinked, sneezing in the sudden bright sunlight. I clambered up on the roof, taking care not to smush my baby sister against the rungs. Once in the open air, I scanned the nearby buildings. Only one of the police snipers was visible from here, and he was at least six stories up.

Patty, meanwhile, was trying another search. "'Chunk of Fortis' . . . here we go. Fortis XC190. It's some meteorite that hit the earth two years ago. There are rumors that being exposed to it gives people increased strength and adrenaline."

"That's cool," I said.

"It also makes them mentally unstable."

"Not so cool."

"Ooh, like that guy from Florida," chimed in Fletcher. "The one who punched the ATM out of the wall? Remember, I sent you that video. People think he was exposed to Fortis too."

"So now we're dealing with superpowered villains. That's fun," I said, doing all I could to convey that it was not fun at all.

I peered across the street. Fifty feet ahead of us and ten feet above, the bald guy was pacing the ledge and ranting, seemingly unaware he was 150 feet off the ground and that a full-grown woman dangled from his right hand. His voice drifted over to me, raspy and angry.

"No more games! I want Superkid here, and I want her to bring me a chunk of Fortis right now, or this chick goes splat!" He shook his hostage for emphasis. She screamed, trying to cling to her captor.

"Hey!" I yelled. "Hey, Bald Guy! STOP!" I waved my arms around, trying to get Baldy's attention. As he turned toward me, I got a look at his face. Veins stood out on his bald scalp, and his skin was beaded with sweat. His pupils were large and jittery. That's not a colorful adjective—his eyes were vibrating like kernels of corn skittering across a hot pan.

"Who are you?" Baldy yelled back.

"Superkid. And her"—I hated myself for saying the next word— "sidekick."

"What?"

I cupped a hand to my mouth. "SUPERKID. AND SIDEKICK."

From the adjacent window, the hostage negotiator raised a megaphone to her mouth. She was in her forties, with limp, dull brown hair cut into the shape of a *Star Wars* Rebel fighter helmet. Oversized old lady sunglasses covered her eyes. Her voice came across the street, no-nonsense and amplified. "Whoever you are, you are interrupting a federal negotiation. Please desist."

"I told you, no more negotiations," said Baldy. "I want my—" He broke off, as if hearing another voice in his head. "Shut up, I can't talk to you and them at the same time. I want some Fortis. Now."

"We'll get whatever you want!" I yelled. "Just put the woman back inside and we can talk."

"Incorrect," said the hostage negotiator. "Put her back inside and *we* can talk."

"Can't we work together on this?" I asked.

"No," came her amplified reply.

"I gotta get over there," I said to Fletcher and Patty. "Release the balloons."

In the alley, Fletcher opened the trunk of the Bentley and pulled out a bunch of shiny helium-filled balloons. He ran to the front of my building, then sent them skyward. They floated up quickly, but across the street, Baldy's patience had finally run out.

"Man, screw this," he said, and released his hold on the hostage.

The woman screamed as she fell. Luckily, the balloons crested the edge of the roof at the same moment. Val's eyes lit up, and she reached for the shiny, floating objects. There was a bass-y *thrum*—

And we catapulted across the rooftop. My boots left twin furrows in the gravel, then Val and I went over the edge. We burst through the cluster of balloons, continuing across the street like an arrow shot from a bow. The hostage was falling right toward us.

"Brace yourself!" I yelled to pretty much everyone involved.

The woman only had a moment to look over, and then Val and I collided with her. We smacked into a fire escape as if we were magnets on a giant fridge.

"How did you—is that a *baby?*" the hostage said in shock.

"She's Superkid," I told her. "You mind hanging on to that railing?"

Once she had a strong hold on the fire escape, I tickled Val's armpits. My sister squealed and demagnetized. We dropped toward the street. Even through the wind whistling past our heads, I could hear the gasps of the watching crowd. Dimly, part of me realized that every camera below was now pointed our way. I pulled the air horn from my belt. The street was getting closer by the millisecond. Then, ten feet from becoming concrete jelly, I pressed the air horn button.

The resulting *BLAAAT* made Val jump. There was a familiar, high-pitched *boing*, and our deadly descent came to a stop. My baby sister and I hung before the astonished crowd, levitating a few feet off the ground.

Everyone burst into spontaneous applause and cheers. This time I was ready. I formed several superhero poses while people snapped pictures and yelled out questions.

"One at a time!" I shouted. "We're happy to answer all your questions, just—ahhh!!" Val had spotted the balloons again. She cranked up her EM field, shooting us straight up into the sky.

"What's happening?" Fletcher said over the headset. "Did you do something?"

"No, she did," I said as we passed the hostage and continued upward. The speed made my eyes water. "She does have a mind of her own, you know."

Patty's voice came through my earpiece. "Try tickling her again."

I complied, tickling Val's ribs and legs. She squealed, and our ascent stopped. We hung in the air for a moment, twenty stories off the ground, then gravity took hold, and we began to drop back down.

"Nona-ba," said my sister in annoyance, turning up her EM field and sending us skyward again.

"What are you doing?" I said to her. "We're missing our first press conference. Bad baby, bad baby!" I tickled her again. We dropped briefly, but then she *boinged* and we went upward some more. Up and down we went, ricocheting between the disappearing balloons and the adoring public below.

"I know you guys are having fun up there," said Fletcher into my earpiece, "but Baldy is getting away."

I looked down at the Rexall Orderlies building. After the psycho had dropped his hostage, it seemed a couple cops had burst into the apartment and tried to grab him. There had been a brief struggle, during which Baldy threw them around the apartment like feather pillows. Now he was parkour running up the building's fire escape. He somersaulted over a railing, leapt eight feet into the air, and pulled himself onto the rooftop. He was about fifty feet below us now.

"Not if we can help it," I said, and blew a raspberry on the back of Val's neck. She laughed, cutting off her EM field and dropping us toward the building. I pulled a bag of potato chips from my jacket and ripped them open. Chips fluttered around us like salt-and-vinegar-flavored leaves, and my baby sister recoiled in surprise.

Thrum. There was a bass-y vibration as Val magnetized. We shot sideways, a mere six feet off the rooftop, and smacked into a large metal vent with a loud, sonorous *clang*. We hung there, stuck like a dart in a board. "Well, that needs some work," I said.

Even worse, the sound of our "landing" drew the attention of Baldy. He turned toward us. His eyes were two vibrating eight balls in a sweaty shaved skull. I was close enough now to see the details of his multiple tattoos, and they were not bunnies and kittens. Upon seeing us, he grinned, revealing four or five silver teeth.

"Who are you supposed to be?" he called out to me. "Magneto's kid cousin?"

"Nice. Solid burn," I told him. "What does that make you, Professor X with roid rage?" Not the best comeback, I know, but you try inventing a witty put-down when you're stuck to the side of an air vent. I made a mental note to work up some all-purpose superhero quips for the future. For now, I had to stay on track. "We're here to bring you in. Surrender, and you won't be hurt."

Baldy laughed. "*You're* gonna hurt *me*? Good luck with that."

"All right, you asked for it." I tickled the bottoms of Val's feet. She wheezed a laugh and we abruptly dropped off the air vent. It was only a few feet, but I slipped and fell on my butt. Very heroic. Val bounced on my chest, but my tailbone absorbed all the damage.

"This costume needs more padding," I groaned.

"Can you please make an effort to look cooler?" Fletcher asked via headset. "There are, like, two news choppers streaming this on live TV."

"Now you tell me," I groaned, pushing myself to my feet.

Patty broke in. "Robbie, Patty again. How exactly do you plan to subdue this man?"

"I have one or two ideas," I said, raising my fists. "But suggestions are always welcome."

Baldy laughed as he saw my battle stance. "Wow, you really wanna do this, huh? Okay, kid. School is now in session."

Before I could respond or even think, he ran at me. I spun, protecting Val with my arms. *Bam bam bam*—Baldy drilled my shoulders and back with a flurry of super-hard punches, then topped it off with a shove. I stumbled toward the wall and *CRACK*—the visor of my motorcycle helmet split. My brain rang like a church bell on Sunday. The spots where Baldy had hit me throbbed with pain.

My attacker jerked his chin to the side, cracking at least a half dozen vertebrae. Then he surged forward again.

"Use her EM field!" Patty said frantically.

I fumbled for the air horn at my belt—

And *BLAAAAAT*—I pressed the button. Val startled, and I bent at the waist. There was a *boing*, but instead of flying straight up, my sister launched us into a forward flip. My boots collided with Baldy's chest at about twenty miles per hour, slamming him backward across the rooftop. This time I managed to land upright.

"Yes!" Fletcher crowed in the alley below. "Now *that* is how we superhero!"

But Baldy seemed unfazed. He got to his feet, his facial expression similar to what the sky looks like right before a category five hurricane. "You picked the wrong guy to tangle with, *cabrón*. I'm gonna take you apart, then use your head for a—aaahhh."

He doubled over, clutching his head in pain. When he stood upright, his all-black pupils had ceased jittering and shrunk back down to a normal size and color. He put a hand to his sweaty skull. "What did I—who are you?" He looked at his surroundings, then back at me. "Is that a *baby*?"

"You mean, the one you just tried to punch? Yeah."

"*Mierda*." He squeezed his eyes shut. Pressed the heel of his hand to his forehead. "It's the Fortis, man. Sometimes I wake up and I don't remember where I am. What I've done. One or two times I was covered in blood."

He suddenly seemed to become aware of the hovering news helicopters. He stepped to the edge of the roof, seeing the police cars and crowds below. "Is that for *me*? What'd I do this time?" Tears welled in his eyes. "Did I . . . hurt someone?"

The change in his personality was so striking, I decided to soft-pedal the details for now. "She's fine. We caught her. But the cops might be a teeny bit peeved with you."

Baldy clutched the sides of his skull. "I can't go back inside, man. I can't do that kinda time again." He smacked himself on the head a few times. "Stupid. Stupid, stupid idiot, listening to that *araña*!"

"Take it easy. Who are you talking about?"

"The Phoenix. The one who gave me the Fortis pills, and promised a bunch more if I did one thing for him. That must have been this. Stupid!"

"We all make mistakes," I said soothingly. "Maybe not as big as this, but I'm sure we can figure it out. Let's start with the Phoenix. What do they look like?"

"I don't know. I only met him on Skype. He had a mask and a voice changer." He looked over the edge of the building again. "He's gonna kill me."

"So you had some contact with him. Do you know his email? Phone number?"

He opened his mouth to reply, but at that moment the stairwell door was kicked open. Two officers ran on to the rooftop, guns drawn. Baldy and I raised our hands like people who had seen plenty of cop shows. A woman exited the stairwell. The hostage negotiator. Now that her face wasn't covered by a megaphone, I could see she had a grim expression beneath her mirrored sunglasses. She wore a trim government-issue business suit, and a gold badge hung from her lapel.

"Emilio Valdez," she said. Her voice had the flat affect of a humorless gym teacher. "I am Agent Bergerschmidt, Department of Homeland Security. Yes, I said Bergerschmidt—it's a family name. You are under arrest for kidnapping, terrorism, and two counts of assaulting an officer. We would prefer if you came quietly, but we will use force if necessary. What is your response?"

I cleared my throat, remembering to deepen my voice. "Uh, ma'am? We were kind of in the middle of something. Can you give us five minutes?"

Agent Bergerschmidt held out a finger toward me. "Do not interfere more than you already have, young man."

Baldy—or rather, Emilio—shook his head. "I can't go back." He began to edge toward the lip of the roof.

"Whoa whoa whoa!" I said. "Don't do that. I told you, we can figure this out. Just tell us how to find the Phoenix." I turned to the federal agent. "Right? Tell him we can figure this out!"

"We are not in cahoots, young man," was her response. "Emilio, stop moving."

"It's too late." He stepped up on the ledge.

"Anything can be fixed," I told him. "But not if you do that, right? Look at us. You wanna scar this baby for life?"

Emilio looked away from the street below him and met my eyes. Gone was the sharklike, animal deadness from before. Now the only emotions I saw on his face were pain and regret. He looked at Val, wavering briefly—

Then Emilio stepped off the roof.

There was a terrible moment of silence, followed by a rough, metal *clang*. All four of us ran to the edge of the roof and peered over. Emilio had landed on a fire escape balcony two stories down. His left leg was bent at an angle that screamed "six to eight weeks in a cast, minimum."

"Take him into custody," Bergerschmidt said crisply to the two policeman. While they started down to Emilio, she turned to me. "Now then. Who are you? How did you fly through the air like that?"

I put a little distance between us. "You planning to arrest me, too?"

"Not if you cooperate," she said. "But judging by the sound of your voice, that will involve a call to your parents or guardians."

So there it was. At best, Val and I would be taken downtown, unmasked, and my parents would learn the truth. At worst . . . well, I had heard the stories about juvenile detention, and none of them were titled "Happy Fun Times with My New Buddies." If I wanted to continue the life of a superhero, there was only one way down from the building.

So I gave Agent Bergerschmidt a little shrug, and jumped off the roof.

I made sure to choose the side with no fire escapes. By this point, I was getting used to the sudden, gut-wrenching drop of free fall. Instead of pure blind terror, I now had the occasional flash of rational thought. I had one such flash now:

We have to do something about Fortis.

Patty had said Fortis was a meteorite. Somehow this Phoenix

person had gotten ahold of it, or maybe part of it, and given some to Emilio in pill form. That meant other people might have some too. And if they all reacted like Emilio had, then we were in for some real problems.

Before I got any further on that train of thought, though, I hit the air horn. Val startled at the loud blare, cranking up her EM field and decreasing our plummet to a lazy, dandelion-seed-like drift. A stiff breeze nudged us into a side alley. As soon as we touched ground, I ducked under an awning so the news helicopters couldn't find us. Making sure no one was watching, I removed both of our helmets and my leather duster. Maybe it was the stress, but I was sweating like my uncle Carter when Aunt Laurie wants to know who ate her pecan sandies.

Yegor pulled the Bentley into the mouth of the alley. "Come on!" Fletcher yelled to me through the open passenger door. "The choppers still don't know where you went, so put a wiggle on."

I jogged down the alley and buckled Val in her car seat before she could complain. As I hopped in the passenger seat, Fletcher knocked on the soundproofed privacy screen. Yegor put the car into drive.

"Not too shabby for our first outing," said Fletcher as the Bentley merged on to the 110. "We saved the hostage, stopped the bad guy, and had a killer exit moment. Much better than those *Amazing Spider-Man* movies."

"Well, I call it lunacy," said Patty with a disapproving frown. "Fighting adult criminals, jumping off buildings—what if you hadn't been able to trigger Val's power?"

"We've been testing for weeks, and she's never not done it," I said. "And I didn't really want to end our first mission in handcuffs."

"Exactly," Fletcher agreed. "So, what are we getting to celebrate? Milkshakes? In-N-Out? Anything you want, it's on me."

Val grunted, and a sharp, familiar scent reached our nostrils. I leaned over to sniff my baby sister and nearly gagged. "Wherever it is, we better make sure they have a bathroom," I said. "Superkid just took a super-dump."

Dirty diapers aside, the next two weeks were the best of my entire life.

Once the footage of our hostage rescue and subsequent escape hit the Internet, people went nuts. There were no more questions about whether or not Val's powers were a special effect. She was the world's first real superhero. Now everyone had to figure out how to deal with that information.

For nearly fourteen days we were the number one story in the news cycle. Fan clubs were formed. Scientists debated the evolutionary implications. Talking heads (such as my nemesis Fran Caulder) discussed the pros and cons of Val's existence every night. In her case, naturally, it was all cons. There were parody videos, opinion pieces, Internet memes, fake Twitter accounts, and Auto-Tuned viral songs. We had more online followers than the president. Websites around the world treated us like celebrities. *Time* magazine dubbed Val "The Poster Child of the Superhero Generation." Even Ben & Jerry's got in on the action, creating an ice cream flavor called "Superkid 'Scream" (which was basically pralines 'n' cream with a purple blackberry ribbon).

But the coolest development was that we actually started helping people. Now that we felt confident about using Val's powers, it seemed like there was no end to the problems we could solve. We helped a beached whale back into the ocean, we rescued a toddler from a downed power line, we pulled two people from a wrecked car on the 5, and we stopped a shoplifter at the mall. We even found time to get a cat out of a palm tree. The only two downsides were that we could only fight crime when my parents were at work, and we couldn't do good during Val's naps. (She was still taking two a day.)

In between missions, Fletcher and Patty tried to find out more information about this "Phoenix" who had supposedly hired Emilio. But besides a few amateur comics and many references to Jean Grey, their Internet searches came up empty. It was like the person didn't exist.

"Maybe we scared him off," Fletcher suggested. "Or her. Could be a female. Whoever it is, maybe this Phoenix person saw us in action and was all 'No more breaking bad for me.'"

"I concur," said Patty. "If he/she was truly a criminal mastermind, I assume we would find some evidence of their existence."

"Unless they wanted to disappear," I pointed out. "The best villains, they don't have to showboat. They operate behind the scenes. Incognito. Like the Queen in *Snow White*."

"Which means there's nothing we can do about it," said Fletcher. "So why not focus on other things? Like all these help requests that are piling up." He showed me a line of new messages in the Superkid inbox.

But I shook my head. "Things have been going too well. Anytime a superhero relaxes in the comics, boom! That's when the bad guy shows up. We have to be prepared."

"And I propose that you watch too many movies," said Patty. "Real life doesn't have plot twists."

And yet, that was exactly what I found when Yegor dropped me home later that afternoon. I let myself in the front door, calling out: "Shelby? Val? Anyone know what we're having for dinner?"

Getting no response, I went to the kitchen and grabbed some pretzel thins and hummus. I continued into the family room to watch some Netflix, but froze in the doorway.

Brynn and my dad sat on the couch. Val was clutched protectively between them. She looked perfectly content, but my dad's face was about two shades redder than normal and Brynn's cheeks were streaked with dried tears. Crap.

In the corner of the room stood an adult man wearing a black suit, an earpiece, and a pistol at his hip. Everything about him screamed "Federal Agent." And in a chair across from my parents sat the hostage negotiator I'd last seen on the rooftop two weeks ago. Today she wore a dark blue business suit with a white button-down underneath. Her limp brown hair clung to her head like a salad bowl and her thin lips were set in a frown.

Double crap.

"Good afternoon, Robert," she said in a crisp, clinical voice. "Won't you sit down and join us?"

I swallowed the pretzel-hummus wad in my mouth. It went a couple inches down my esophagus and then screeched to a halt. It felt like there was a baseball in my chest, but I played it cool. "Actually," I said, my voice raspy, "could I get some water first? Wrong tube."

I turned, frantically thinking that I could crawl out the kitchen window. I'd call a Lyft and hide out at Fletcher's until I figured out how to explain my superhero exploits to my parents. A letter seemed the best bet, sent from a place very, very far away. But the agent in the corner had somehow crossed the room and was now blocking my only exit.

"There is water over here," the agent—Bulgurmeister? Strudelviesse? I remembered there was food in her name—said. "Join us."

The fed before me folded his arms. I had no choice but to slink over and sit. My dad glared at me like there was lava shooting out of his eyes. I vowed never to look in his direction again. Maybe if I played dumb, there was a way out of this. After all, it's not like they could throw me in prison. Could they?

I picked up a glass of water and took a big gulp, relieved to feel the wad of pretzels finally descend toward my stomach. "What's, uh . . . what's all this about?" I said, unable to keep my voice from wavering.

"No more lies, Robbie," my dad said. "We know what you've been up to with your sister, and we are very, very, VERY—"

The agent in charge held up her hand. "If I may, Mr. Rampino." My dad sat back on the couch and crossed his legs. "Robert, I'm Agent Bergerschmidt. It's a family name. We've been tracking your movements since our meeting in downtown Los Angeles two weeks ago. You and your . . . associates have employed some clever tactics, but nobody evades Homeland Security forever. We like to hunt."

"Okay," I said. "What . . . exactly . . . do you know?"

"Everything," she responded. "But there's a large aspect of this I believe *you* don't know. Before we get into that, however, I'd like hear your side of things."

I risked another look at my parents. My dad still resembled a boiled lobster, but Brynn stared back at me beseechingly.

"Please, honey," she said, her voice creased with emotion. "We just want to know the truth. Did someone force you into this? Did they threaten you? Maybe offer you money?"

Geez, what a naive weakling they took me for. Like I would risk my baby sister's well-being for a little bit of money. Any remaining thoughts I had of playing dumb were abandoned. I sighed. "No. This was all me."

"I knew it." My dad got to his feet, unable to corral his thoughts. "Robbie, what you've done—the danger to your sister—you're grounded, that's number one. Number two, you're going to see a doctor. A psychiatrist. Number three—"

"Dad." I got up too and laid a hand on his shoulder. The touch shook him out of his stuttering rage. "Can you let me explain? Please?" He blinked at me like a stunned fish. For the first time, I realized we were nearly the same size. Brynn took his hand in hers. "It's okay, Mike," she said. "Let him talk."

My dad sank back to the couch. And I began to talk.

I'll save you the blow-by-blow account of what followed. It was pretty similar to the reveal talk I'd had with Fletcher, only with more apologizing and much more groveling. Brynn and my dad demanded proof, so I demonstrated Val's bouncing ability, then I walked them through all our exploits. I explained everything that Patty had learned about my baby stepsister's ability, and how it worked like a protective instinct. I emphasized how much I'd hated lying, and how I'd only done it to keep my parents from more stress. The yelling was minimal, which I took to be a good sign. By the end of my exposition dump, my father had returned to a semi-normal color and I was able to look my parents in the eye again.

"Well, that lines up with our timeline," said Agent Bergerschmidt, flipping closed a small brown moleskin notebook. I'd almost forgotten she was in the room. "But there is a lot more the three of you don't know. I'm afraid you'll have to come with us."

We've all heard of performance-enhancing drugs. Barry Bonds, Lance Armstrong, Roger Clemens—pretty much every professional athlete seems to have used or encountered someone who uses them. But did you know the practice of doping before the big game goes back three thousand *years*? The Greeks in the very first Olympics drank opium juice, used hallucinogens, even chowed down on testicles in their search for better performance.

For better or worse, our methods have evolved since then. In 100 AD, Roman gladiators drank strychnine so they could ignore their injuries. By the late 1800s, French cyclists had discovered cocaine, and mixed it with wine to create a fun sports beverage that would keep them pedaling all night long. And of course nowadays athletes use everything from designer steroids to human growth hormones to copious amounts of Red Bull to give them an advantage.

The latest forward leap in body-enhancement technology, Agent Bergerschmidt told us, was exotic radiation. Instead of changing the nature of the body through short-term chemical reactions, this method involved mutating human genes. Currently there were two types of radiation therapy—cell modification and germline modification. Cell therapy used radioactive isotopes, taken in pill form, to directly modify the body in specific areas, such as leg muscles or lungs. Germline radiation modding, however, targets the genes in an embryo. The genetic changes are born with the subject, affect the entire body, and can even be passed on to future generations.

"Although it should go without saying, I will say it anyway—both of these methods are highly illegal. Not to mention dangerous." Agent Bergerschmidt stood at the opposite end of a conference table. At the other end, Fletcher, Patty, my entire family, and I sat huddled together. We were in a windowless room on the tenth floor of a Los Angeles federal building. Val was snoozing in her car seat in the corner. Agent Bergerschmidt had brought us here directly from our home in Pasadena, in our very own federal van. We'd arrived in this room to find Patty and Fletcher had been rounded up as well. For the last twenty minutes, Bergerschmidt had been giving us an overly detailed history of performance enhancers.

"The most dangerous form of performance enhancing radiation we've encountered," she continued, "is derived from this." The agent clicked a remote, and a computer animation re-creation showed a meteorite crashing into a mountainside. "The meteorite Fortis XC190. It crashed in West Virginia two years ago, and it was quickly determined that the radiation from this interstellar rock could amplify human strength and endurance." Onscreen, a microscopic bit of rock was placed next to a single cell. Within moments the cell doubled in size and grew spikes.

"So Fortis makes people Hulk out?" asked Fletcher. "Awesome."

"Not awesome," said Bergerschmidt sternly. "The meteorite was sold via a black market auction to an unknown buyer a year ago. Since then, cases like Emilio Valdez have been popping up all over.

Incredibly strong, incredibly crazy people who have been exposed to Fortis, but can't tell us how they got it."

I raised my hand. "They forgot? Or they never knew?"

"Unclear," said the agent. "Whoever's distributing Fortis, they're very good at covering their tracks. And they have begun to refine the meteorite's effects." She clicked her remote, showing an amateur video of a muscular tank-top-wearing man punch a row of cinder blocks with his bare fists. Despite the snap, crackle, and pop of his own hand bones, he kept going until the blocks were dust and pebbles.

"As we saw with Emilio, these effects only last a short time. Unless, however, the Fortis is administered during the *formation* of a genetic code. If that happens, the changes can become permanent." Behind her played an animated video of a DNA strand. A yellow-gray chip of Fortis entered the frame, bonded to the DNA, and the whole strand became yellow and spiky.

Bergerschmidt clicked to the next video, which had a *TOP SECRET* title superimposed in the center of the screen. "Thankfully," she continued, "we were able to obtain a small amount of the meteorite for study." A series of shots showed several mouse fetuses being injected with some kind of irradiated Fortis juice. The resulting adult mice were shown generating electrical fields, running on treadmills until they became superfast blurs, and sneezing holes in the bars of their solid steel cages. All of us watched the footage with slack jaws.

"Didn't you guys watch *Jurassic World*?" Patty asked angrily. "Creating super-mice breaks every law of evolution and scientific responsibility!"

"You're right," said Bergerschmidt. "But we can't let our enemies, foreign or domestic, perfect such techniques without at least understanding how they work, and learning how to protect ourselves from them. The unpredictable nature of the meteorite's properties has, thus far, kept anyone from proceeding to germline human trials. With, we believe, one exception." She looked at Val, who sighed and shifted in her sleep.

Brynn's voice wavered in shock. "That's what made my baby like this? She was exposed to some . . . radioactive space rock?!"

"We believe so. We obtained a blood sample from her pediatrician, and our tests confirm her DNA has been mutated by Fortis. On the upside, it does not appear to be actively hurting her."

"Not hurting her?!" said my dad loudly. "What if she magnetizes herself and sticks to a passing plane? Or erases her own brain and forgets how to breathe??"

Bergerschmidt was unruffled. "All our testing trials have shown that the mice who survive the in vitro treatments live healthy, semi-normal lives."

"Semi-normal," Brynn repeated. Not caring that her daughter was still asleep, she lifted Val out of the car seat and cuddled her close. "Well, that puts me right at ease."

"How could this have happened?" asked Patty. "You created the super-mice through in vitro injection. I assume something like that couldn't have occurred without Robbie's mom noticing." Brynn shook her head vigorously.

Bergerschmidt clicked a pen and began reading a checklist from her moleskin notebook. "Ms. Cooper-Rampino. During your pregnancy, did you use any recreational drugs?"

"Of course not," said my stepmom.

"What about your doctors or nurses? Was there any suspicious behavior there?"

My dad and Brynn shook their heads vigorously.

Bergerschmidt read off the next few items. "Kidnapping, poisoning, diet . . . did you take any supplements when you were pregnant? Prescription drugs of any kind?"

Brynn's look of confusion suddenly cleared. "Prenatal vitamins.

But my doctor recommended those."

"I see." Bergerschmidt made another note. I peered over to see what she had written, but she tilted the notebook away from me.

"Is that bad?" asked my dad. "I thought everyone took prenatal vitamins these days."

"Indeed they do. Which makes them a particularly prime target for sabotage." She placed the form back in her folder. "Irradiating your vitamins is the most likely way for Val to have been exposed to Fortis in vitro," Bergerschmidt said.

"Irradiating?" My stepmother looked horrified. "Someone irradiated me when I was pregnant? How could they do that?"

The agent shrugged. "They could grind up the meteorite, place a chunk of it close to your pills, even paint the isotope directly onto your medication. The important thing is, we believe this is the man responsible."

She clicked her remote again, but nothing happened. "*This* is the man responsible," she repeated, but still got no response from her remote. "Hold on a second." She shook the device, then tapped her computer keyboard.

"Is it the remote battery?" asked Fletcher.

Bergerschmidt shook her head, making sure all the cables were connected. "I'm hitting space; it should play," she said.

Fletcher got up and leaned over her computer. "Try rebooting PowerPoint."

"Why would that do it?" the agent asked.

"It's a computer, nobody knows."

I lost my patience. "Can't you just tell us who did this?!"

They both looked at me as the PowerPoint program restarted. Quickly, Bergerschmidt clicked through the slides and videos we'd already seen, until she landed on the mug shot of an intense, glaring gray-haired man in his fifties.

"Armin Tanzarian," said Bergerschmidt. "Aka the Gampr. That's an Armenian dog." She clicked to the next slide, which was a picture of a large beige-colored canine that was reminiscent of a shepherd and a husky.

"Awww," said Patty. She flushed as we all looked her way. "Sorry. I like dogs."

Bergerschmidt clicked to a surveillance photo of Tanzarian yelling into his cell phone. "The Gampr has had three people killed that we know of. He's also the biggest importer of illegal contraband in California. Prides himself on collecting difficult-to-find items. We think he's the one who bought up the majority of Fortis. Do any of you recognize him?"

She looked around the conference table. Brynn and my dad shook their heads, as did Patty. I made eye contact with Fletcher, who shrugged.

Bergerschmidt was not surprised. "Whoever irradiated your pills—possibly this 'Phoenix' character—he or she almost certainly got their piece of Fortis from Tanzarian."

"So what are you waiting for?" asked Brynn. "Go arrest him."

"Yeah," agreed Fletcher. "You guys have all those offshore black site prisons. Take him to one of those and waterboard him until he talks."

"Despite what inappropriate films you may have seen, that's not how the United States government works. If we were to arrest Tanzarian for no reason, his lawyers would have the case thrown out. What we need is proof." She began to tidy up her stack of papers. "But if you don't know him, then that's not your concern. For now, all you have to do is head home and keep Val safe."

We were nonplussed by the sudden shift in her tone. "So . . . that's it?" asked my dad.

Bergerschmidt nodded. "We appreciate you all coming in."

"What about Val's powers?" I asked. "Can we still . . . use them?"

"Oh, absolutely not," the agent said as she turned off the projector screen. "Use of her abilities without a permit would be considered a felony offense, and anyone involved would be prosecuted to the full extent of the law." She showed her teeth in what must have been her idea of a smile. It looked painful. "Enjoy the rest of your day, and stay out of trouble."

We did not take her advice.

Five days later, Fletcher, Patty, Val, and I sat in the Grossman's Bentley outside of a mansion in Brentwood. Yegor was behind the wheel, listening to some kind of Russian MMA fight. Because of the soundproofed screen, we couldn't hear him and he couldn't hear us.

"Once more, I would like to state that this is a terrible idea," Patty said.

I was inclined to agree with her. After we'd left the meeting with Bergerschmidt, Fletcher had been incensed. He'd gone on and on about how the government couldn't order us around, and it was dumb to trust the same people who spied on us through our phones.

"But the dumbest part," he had ranted to me over the phone that night, "is that they expect us to sit back and do nothing while Tanzarian uses up the meteorite."

"What else can we do about it?" I asked him.

"What a superhero would do," he'd replied. "We go after Tanzarian ourselves."

I'd blown him off, but the next day he'd shown up at my house with Patty in tow. He already had a whole plan. While Shelby watched Val inside the house (my babysitting privileges had been revoked), we sat on my back patio and he went over his idea.

First he opened his laptop and double-clicked a folder of images. A glamour shot of a huge gaudy mansion appeared onscreen. "This is Tanzarian's house in Brentwood." He tapped the space bar, and the house photo dissolved to a digital three-dimensional rendering that spun around. There was a pool, guest house, and horse stables. "It's a ten-thousand-square foot McMansion, made of stones he had chiseled and imported from Mount Ararat."

"Not very eco-friendly," sniffed Patty.

"That's the least of this guy's crimes," said Fletcher. "He's done all kinds of criminal stuff over the years, but the feds have never been able to make anything stick. If he's got Fortis, I'm betting it's somewhere in his house. There's just one problem."

He tapped another key. Over two dozen pulsing red points lit up all over Tanzarian's property. "His home security is top-of-the-line, better than what my dad has at our place. Infrared cameras, biometric keypads at every entrance, and a minimum of six armed guards patrolling the joint, all of which Tanzarian controls from his phone." Onscreen, an animated bird landed on one windowsill, and the stick-figure guards ran forward to blast it into oblivion.

I was impressed. "How'd you find out all this stuff?"

Fletcher shrugged. "My dad keeps a private investigator on retainer to research his business competitors. Dude was having a slow week, so he agreed do a little digging for me."

"Does he do the animation, too?"

"Oh no, I found that online. FreeAnimatics.com."

"It's impressive research, but what are you proposing?" Patty asked, bringing us both back on track. "Breaking into a criminal kingpin's fortress and stealing his personal belongings definitely goes against Bergerschmidt's recommendations. Not to mention the law."

"We're not breaking in," Fletcher had said with a self-satisfied grin. "I have a way we can stroll right through the front door. One that's tailor-made for a Superkid." He turned his laptop toward us. Onscreen was a Facebook invite to a birthday party taking place that weekend. The banner read *Our Teeny Tanzarian Turns One!*

"The Guyver's got a kid," Fletcher had said. "And he's only three months older than Val."

So now here we were, just a few days later, ready to stroll into the heavily guarded compound of a notorious criminal. Patty was wrong. Calling the idea "terrible" was an understatement.

"It's gonna be fine," Fletcher replied. He was gently wrapping a birthday present, while Patty nervously double-checked files on her laptop. Val sat next to me in her car seat, playing with her squeezy giraffe and blissfully unaware of the danger we were about to place her in. Since I wasn't allowed to be alone with my sister, we'd had to "borrow" her out of her bedroom while she was asleep. I'd left a note in the crib, assuring my dad and Brynn that we'd be back by dinner, but I still felt pretty guilty about it. Fletcher had repeatedly reminded me that we were doing this for Val's protection.

"Just remember why we're here," he continued, as if hearing my thoughts. "Bergerschmidt said she can't arrest this guy without proof, so we're going in there to get her some. Val won't be in danger. It'll take twenty minutes, tops."

I glanced at Tanzarian's house. Two grizzly bear-sized, shades-wearing guards stood at the front gate, checking in guests.

"Tell that to those guys," Patty said. "They look like they stepped out of the movies my dad won't let me watch."

"It's a birthday party for a one-year-old," Fletcher reminded us. "The Glamping won't do anything dangerous in front of his guests.

Will he, cutie-pie? Will he?" He tickled Val's knees, and she gave him a gummy grin.

"It's the Gampr," Patty told him. "At least know the scary nickname of the guy you're trying to rob."

"Gipper, Glamping—whatever the name, he's no match for us," he said. "Is the equipment good to go?"

Patty sighed, but she held up Val's baby carrier. "I placed fiber-optic cameras in the front and back. We'll be recording the whole time. Any problems, and I'll immediately call the cops."

She passed out our two-way radio earpieces and we put them in place. Fletcher turned to me. "Right, let's go over it one more time. Who are you?"

"Marco Haverford," I said.

"And your sister?"

My mind was a blank. We'd spent the last couple days memorizing all this stuff, but I was terrible with names. I made a vague guess. "Beth . . . ?"

"Anne . . ." Patty prompted me, but it still didn't ring any bells.

"Knee," Fletcher finished in frustration. "Beth-an-y Haverford. She takes baby yoga with Tanzarian's daughter." We had guaranteed Bethany wouldn't be able to attend the party by sending Yegor to sabotage her parents' cars. He had been shockingly proficient at it.

"Sorry I didn't go to James Bond school," I told Fletcher. "All these rich people names sound the same."

"I'm going in with you," he decided. "Someone's gotta keep this thing afloat."

Before I could argue, he turned to rap on the privacy screen. It slid down, and Yegor shut off his MMA match. "We're ready," Fletcher told him.

The crew-cutted driver nodded, but Val began to fuss as I unbuckled the straps of her car seat. She began to open and close her chubby fist in the sign for *milk*, something Brynn and my dad had taught her months ago.

"She's hungry," I said. "She should probably eat before we do this." Eleven minutes, a bottle of formula, a container of Cheerios, and a squeezy pouch filled with purple carrots and yams later, I patted Val's back until she gave an impressive burp. I wiped the purple food goatee off her face. Fletcher glared at us the entire time, drumming his fingers impatiently on his knees.

"Okay," I said, lifting Val into the baby carrier. My sister grunted, and a familiar scent wafted into my nostrils. "Actually, now I think she needs a diaper."

Six more minutes passed. Fletcher spent the whole time miming various methods of suicide, but finally Val's booty was cleaned and re-diapered. Once more, we strapped her into the baby carrier.

"*Now* are we ready?" my best friend said testily.

"Actually . . ." Fletcher's face turned bright red, but I cut him off. "It's a joke, dude. Let's roll."

Fletcher, Yegor, and I crossed the street to Tanzarian's mansion. Patty stayed in the Bentley, where she could monitor our progress and feed us information. The grizzly bear guards turned to us as we approached. I couldn't see any gun bulges in their suits, but I knew they were packing.

"Name?" the slightly larger grizzly said to us. He had an iPad in his left hand.

Fletcher nudged me. "Marco Haverford," I said, hefting Val in the baby carrier. "And this is my sister, my chaperone, and my, uh . . . friend." I stared at Fletcher, not sure what to call him.

"Billy," he said in a terrible Irish accent, offering a hand. "Billy O'Bobbins. Of the Baltimore O'Bobbinses. Aren't you lads hot in those suits? It's so hot out here."

Slightly Larger Grizzly ignored him and stared me down. "You and the baby are on the list, but the invitation said all plus-ones had to be cleared in advance."

"Did it say that?" I asked. "My mom sent the RSVP, so . . . isn't there any way we can just duck in? Say hello?"

"I promise not to eat more than one slice o' cake," Fletcher said with a wink. "Unless it's really, really good. Which, let's face it, most b-day cakes usually are not, am I right?"

"Tone down the accent," said Patty over our earpiece transmitters. "You sound like you're auditioning for a part in the next *Leprechaun* movie."

"Copy that," said Fletcher in a more normal voice, then caught himself. "I mean, do you need to copy that? Our invitation? 'Cause we have it right here." He pulled a sweaty, crumpled ball of paper out of his pocket.

Slightly Larger Grizzly pressed a remote, and the front gate began to swing open. "Enjoy the party," he said with the greatest amount of disdain he could muster.

"Nice job," I said out of the side of my mouth as we entered Tanzarian's compound. "Really glad you came along on this."

"We got in, didn't we?" said Fletcher.

We entered the backyard. If you set aside the amazing pool, top-notch landscaping, and gigantic guest house, it actually looked like a pretty typical kid's birthday party. There was a table stacked with presents, a buffet table loaded with food, tacky princess-themed decorations, and clusters of parents making strained small talk.

I placed our wrapped box on the gift table, then Fletcher and I turned to survey the main house. There was a dark-suited gorilla blocking each entrance, and biometric keypads beneath each doorknob. Fletcher's research had been spot-on.

"Please tell me you have a plan for getting past all that," I muttered.

"No sweat," Fletcher said. "We'll just walk over there and—"

"Hellooo!" said a strident, slightly accented voice. A mid-thirties woman in a tight sparkly dress and five-inch heels tottered over to us. In each of her hands was a half-filled champagne flute, which sloshed as she walked. When *The Real Housewives of Brentwood* got made, she would clearly be a prime candidate.

"Polonia Tanzarian," she breathed, offering each of us a bony ring-encrusted hand. "Welcome, welcome, welcome. And who is this precious little angel?" She bent to examine Val.

I cleared my throat. "Uh, Beth. Beth-Anne."

"Bethany," corrected Fletcher.

"Right, Bethany. Beth-Anne's her nickname." I tried to smile. "She's in baby yoga with, uh . . ." I looked at Fletcher, unable to remember the name of Tanzarian's child. He stared back at me, his mind also blank.

"Copenhagen," Patty said over the earpiece. "That's the kid's name."

"Copenhagen!" I said. "He's such a cutie-pie."

"Copenhagen is a girl," said Polonia frostily.

Whoops. I tried to move on. "So, do you guys like that stuff? Yoga? My parents say the teacher is—"

"Do not mention that woman to me," said Polonia, now angry. "She may be a respected yogi from wherever, but when that hussy wanted a raise, my husband had her *deported*."

Yikes. "Sounds like . . . a guy who knows what he wants," said Fletcher.

"Oh, he is." The woman turned, waving her hand like she was shooing away a mosquito. "Armin! *Aystegh ari!*"

And there he was. Crossing the patio toward us, power and menace radiating from his six-foot frame. The Gampr himself, the owner of the meteorite that had turned my baby sister into a freak of nature. The criminal we had come to rob.

Armin Tanzarian.

The criminal kingpin wore a suit that, if sold, could have fed a middle-class neighborhood for a month. A gold necklace hung around his thick tan neck, and several gold rings adorned his strong fingers. An actual gampr dog trotted beside him, a steel choke chain cinched around its throat. Its huge, shaggy head stood well above Tanzarian's waist.

When they got within five feet of us, the dog barked. His mouth was large enough to swallow Val in one bite. She whimpered, but thankfully didn't crank up her EM field.

"Awww," said Patty over our earpieces. Then: "Sorry."

Tanzarian yanked on the dog's choke chain. "Please excuse Jaws." His voice was thickly accented, and surprisingly pleasant. "These parties, for him they are murder."

"Who can blame him?" I said. "There's a few people I'd like to bark at too, buddy." I reached out a hand to pet him, but Jaws snapped, nearly leaving me with a stump.

"Quick little fella, isn't he?" said Fletcher.

"Indeed." Tanzarian smiled like a shark. "Thank you for attending our little party, young gentlemen, and . . . ?" He looked at Yegor curiously.

"Our chaperon," said Fletcher cheerily. "He's an introvert. Right, Yegor?"

"Mmmm," Yegor grunted.

"Uh-oh," I said, bending forward to sniff Val. "Yup, this diaper's dead. You mind if I use your bathroom?"

"Of course," said Tanzarian, gesturing to the guest house. "Our pool house is very well-appointed."

"Negative!" said Patty over our earpieces. "His office is in the main house."

Fletcher stepped forward. "Actually, I need to use that one." He placed a hand on his stomach. "Too much Taco Bell for lunch. Bye!" He hustled off to the bathroom, giving me a significant look.

"Sorry about that," I said with a strained laugh. "I told him not to eat that crap."

"Never mind," said Polonia. "Armin, let the poor boy and his sister use the house restroom."

Tanzarian hesitated, giving me the chance to jump in. "Thanks, that would be a huge help," I said. "Val's number twos, they're more like tens."

Polonia frowned. "Who is Val?"

Double whoops. "Did I say Val?"

"You did," said Tanzarian.

"Oh, *Val.*" I tried not to break out into a flop sweat. "That's just another one of . . . this one's, uh . . ."

"BETHANY," said Patty in my ear.

"Bethany's nicknames," I finished. "'Poopy Val,' we call her."

Tanzarian beckoned over one of his dark-suited gorillas. This one had a cheek scar the length of a butcher knife. "Kodje, please escort this young man to the ground-floor washroom." Tanzarian smiled. "And your chaperone, he may stay here and sample the *nazook*." He turned to Yegor, who grunted in an affirmative sort of manner.

Kodje took me by the arm, practically dragging both me and Val to the main house. He pressed his thumb to the biometric keypad, then escorted us to a marble-lined bathroom with a thick oak door.

"Shoot, you know what?" I said, improvising madly. "I left the baby wipes in the car. You wait here, and I'll go—"

Kodje opened a drawer, revealing a brand-new box of wipes. I refrained from making a face. "You guys. You think of everything."

Reluctantly, I went inside and locked the door. "I'm in the house, but the guard's right outside the door!" I whispered. "Suggestions?"

"We gotta distract 'em," Fletcher said from the pool house bathroom. "Patty, it's time for Plan B."

"Are you nuts? But we didn't even test it!"

"Do it!" Fletcher hissed.

In the Bentley, Patty moaned in extreme worry. I heard her rummage through a bag until she found what she was looking for—a gray remote. "I hope this doesn't kill anyone," she said, then pressed the button.

The present we'd dropped on the gift table exploded. Fireworks—chrysanthemums, comets, even a spinner—burst through the wrapping paper and sizzled through the backyard patio. Guests screamed and dropped to the ground. Birthday packages caught fire. The gorilla guards pulled their pistols, and ran to protect the Tanzarians.

Kodje unholstered his own gun and looked into the backyard, but he didn't leave. I had to take him out myself. I opened the bathroom door, placing my fingers under Val's armpits. He turned to face us.

"Tickle, tickle, tickle," I said in a high-pitched voice. Val squealed, sending out an EM burst. Kodje was slammed backward, his skull cracking against the marble staircase banister. He looked at me, confused, then crumpled to the floor, unconscious.

I dropped his gun into a vase and dragged his limp, heavy body into the bathroom. Val fussed as I bent over, kicking her chubby legs in annoyance. "Shhh," I told her. "We're trying to be stealthy here. Okay, guys, the guard is down. Now how do I find the Gampr's office?"

In the Bentley, Patty pulled up a PDF of Tanzarian's house blueprints. These had been surprisingly easy to obtain from the local city hall. "Head to the south wing," she told me.

I made my way quietly through the house, with Val babbling loudly the whole time. Thankfully, everyone was still dealing with the detonating fireworks outside and couldn't hear her. I reached a long hallway, seeing at least eight doors stretch out before me.

"Which room is it?" I asked Patty.

But I didn't get an answer, because at that moment, Tanzarian opened the door to the pool house bathroom. "Hey!" said Fletcher over my earbud. "I could have been pooping here." There were rustling sounds as he was hauled onto the backyard patio by a guard.

"Where is Kodje?" I heard Tanzarian say to someone. "You, watch this one. You, come with me."

"He's coming to look for you," said Patty.

"Oh, you think?" I said sarcastically. Quickly, I opened doors to check the various rooms. A walk-in wine cellar, a games room, an indoor gym, even a ten-seat movie theater. "Dang," I said. "I can't decide if I hate this guy or I want to be him."

The last door opened into a corner office. It had nice wood furniture, a stone fireplace, and lots of stuffed dead animals. Nothing that looked like a hiding place for files. "Found it," I said. "But I don't see any file storage. He doesn't even have a computer."

"It must be hidden," said Patty. I heard the computer keys clicking as she zoomed in on the office part of the blueprints. "Here we go.

There are extra support beams on the northwest wall, probably for a safe or a panic room."

I approached the wall, pressing all over. There was a soft *click*, and a wall panel slid back, revealing a brushed-steel door with a biometric keypad. "Secret door, we have a secret door!" I said. "There's a keypad, though."

"What's the brand name?" said Patty.

"Uh . . . Colonnade," I read off the panel. Val chirped, so I bounced up and down to soothe her.

"Okay, give me a minute." I could hear Patty's fingers quickly Googling on her laptop. "Safety features, and . . . bingo. The door unlocks if you overload the panel with electricity."

"And how do I do that?" I said. "I'm a kid, not a computer hacker."

"You have an electromagnetic superhero strapped to your chest," Fletcher muttered from the backyard. "*Use* her."

I unbuckled the baby carrier, sitting Val in front of the steel door. I lightly scratched her bare feet, making her shiver. There was a low-pitched *thrum*, and she slid across the wood floor, sticking to the door. She gave me a gummy grin.

Still magnetized, she began to crawl up the metal door. I tried to pull her off, but it was like bending a stone statue. "No Spider-Man-ing right now. Stop it." She ignored me. It was time to pull out the big guns. "Peekaboo. PeekaBOO!" Nothing. I made a scary face. "Rawwwr!"

Val popped off the door in surprise, landing in my arms. Her lower lip jutted out. Her face screwed up in a pre-meltdown. "No, no, no," I tried to soothe her. "It was just to get you off the door, see? Big brother's not scary."

I made a few goofy faces, but froze when I felt a heavy round object press into the back of my skull. It was the barrel of an automatic pistol, and it was clutched in the fist of Armin Tanzarian. I turned, seeing his eyes burning with dark rage.

"Interesting place for a diaper change," he said. He used the gun to gesture that I should come with him. I obeyed.

Outside, Copenhagen's birthday party was a disaster zone. Fireworks had stopped spitting from our Trojan present, but the rest of the gift table was in ashes. The food table had been knocked over. Several guests were huddled behind patio furniture, shielding their young children. Others ran around, demanding to know what was happening from anyone who would listen. Yegor was held at gunpoint by two guards, while Fletcher had been forced to his knees. He was being held by the back of the neck by a massive guard covered in scary-looking tattoos.

Tanzarian shoved me onto the back patio, his pistol pressed against my spine. I held Val in my arms, bouncing her slightly so she wouldn't freak out.

"It's okay, we'll be okay," I said, probably more for myself than her.

Taking one look at the chaos in his backyard, Tanzarian removed the pistol from my back and fired two bullets into the pool.

Everybody froze. "Party over," the Gampr said menacingly. "Your gift bags are by the front exit."

He didn't need to ask twice. The party guests scooped up their kids and hustled for the gate. Each of them dutifully grabbed a gift bag as they left. Within two minutes, the only people left on the patio were me, Val, Fletcher, and eight gun-toting maniacs.

"Oh my God, oh my God, oh my God," Patty buzzed in my ear. "You guys have to get out of there. Use Val's powers or something, but—"

Tanzarian plucked the transmitter out of my ear and inspected it. Patty's voice could still be heard, faintly freaking out. Then he flicked the earpiece into his hot tub.

"Move," he said, gesturing with his pistol toward Fletcher and Yegor. Once we reached them, he forced me to my knees. His gun stayed on us the entire time.

"Armin!" Polonia weaved across the patio toward us, Copenhagen on her hip. Whatever good looks the criminal and his wife had did not seem to have been passed on to their chubby offspring. "It is your daughter's birthday. For once can you not stop working?"

"These boys set off fireworks at my home," Tanzarian said, panning the gun between us. "They were attempting to steal from me."

Polonia's expression grew even angrier as she looked at me. "*You* ruined my baby's party? Do what you want with them," she said, turning back to her husband and kissing him on the cheek. "Just make sure the police can't identify the bodies."

I swallowed as our last potential savior went back inside the house. "We weren't stealing!" I said to Tanzarian. "We were just looking for the meteorite."

"You and everyone else," he said. "Who sent you? Homeland Security? FBI?'"

"You think we came off that professional?" said Fletcher. "Awesome."

"Do not play with me!" barked the Gampr. "I want to know who told you about me, or your day will become . . . messy."

I made eye contact with Fletcher. He shook his head slightly, but I wasn't sure how else we could get out of this situation. I had no chip bags, my airhorn was back in the Bentley, and I had a good feeling that any tickling I tried to instigate would result in me being shot.

Tanzarian grew tired of waiting. He placed two fingers to his lips, whistling sharply. "Jaws!" he yelled. "*Ari!*"

A large tornado of teeth and fur came barreling across the patio. The gampr (the dog one) skidded to a halt next to its owner. It barked once, spraying foamy spittle and revealing long yellow fangs that had no doubt inspired the animal's name.

Tanzarian clipped the choke chain on to Jaws's leash, winding the length around his right hand until there was only a couple feet free. "Here's how this will go," he said. "I will ask a question. If I do not like the answer, Jaws will take a toe from the baby."

At that point, I was wishing Val weren't the only one in diapers. "I told you," I said, trying to keep my voice steady. "We're not with anybody. We just want to know who irradiated my—"

Tanzarian dropped a loop of the choke chain, and Jaws leapt forward. The animal's teeth clacked together a mere two feet from my baby sister's bare feet. Val screamed. Whether she was too terrified to use her powers or whether she needed to fall off a building to stay motivated, I don't know. I only know that she pressed her face against me and did nothing.

"I cannot hold the chain forever," said Tanzarian. "So answer. Who told you about my business??"

"We read about you online!" said Fletcher. "It's not like your career choice is some big secret."

Tanzarian let out another loop of the choke chain. The gampr jumped forward again. Its teeth were now mere inches from us. I could its barking breath on my hands. I tried to move my baby sister away, but with the pool at my back there was no place for us to go. I wasn't about to lose any digits to protect Bergerschmidt.

"Okay!" I shouted over the barking, slavering dog. "We heard about you from—"

BOOM!

The backyard gate was knocked off its hinges by a battering ram, and a dozen SWAT team officers ran onto the patio with their weapons drawn. There was a lot of shouting at the guards, but thankfully Tanzarian didn't let go of the choke chain. He assessed the situation, then calmly nodded to his men. As one, they set down their weapons and raised their hands over their heads. One SWAT officer took charge of Jaws, while another handcuffed Tanzarian and read him his Miranda rights. The criminal kept his eyes on me the entire time, not breaking his gaze until they shoved him out of the gate. I sighed in relief when he was gone.

I stood, the kettle drumbeat of my heart finally beginning to slow. Val gave a shuddering breath. Fletcher ran over, wrapping both of us in a bear hug. "Dude, I am so sorry," he said. "If I had any idea he'd do something like that—"

"But you did," said a gruff, monotone voice. Two SWAT officers stepped aside, and Agent Bergerschmidt walked toward us. She was in yet another bland business suit, and her eyes were covered in mirrored sunglasses. "I informed you both what Tanzarian was capable of. And still, you chose to come on this very ill-advised, very illegal excursion. Congratulations. You just cost the taxpayers of this city four hundred thousand dollars."

"How did you know we were here?" I said.

"Patty emailed me an hour ago," the agent said crisply. The girl stepped out from behind Bergerschmidt, blushing a deep red.

"You emailed her *before* we went in?" asked Fletcher. "Thanks for having our back, you Judas."

"Consider yourselves lucky she did so," said Bergerschmidt. "Had she waited two minutes more, you three would have been dog kibble."

"And we appreciate it," I said. "But more important—we found that evidence you were looking for."

BZZZZZ! The blade of the Homeland Security engineer's rotary saw cut through the last bolt on Tanzarian's panic room door. Fletcher, Patty, Bergerschmidt, me, and at least a half dozen Homeland Security agents watched from the hallway as the heavy steel plate fell to the parquet wood floor with a massive *thud*.

"Holy ghost of Marie Curie," breathed Patty.

Bergerschmidt shined a flashlight into the panic room. There was a small desk, a rack of hard drives, a high-end computer console, and on the back wall, a reinforced glass case containing a blue-green rock the size of a suitcase. It radiated a strange shimmery light.

"What did I tell you?" crowed Fletcher. "We found Fortis, baby!"

I turned to Bergerschmidt. "Now do you have enough evidence to locate the Phoenix?"

"Perhaps," she said, holstering her flashlight. "But it could take days or even weeks to sort through all the information here."

"No need to thank us," said Fletcher sarcastically.

"Don't worry, I won't," she replied shortly. "This crime scene's a jurisdictional nightmare. Especially since you broke the law to uncover it."

"You're the one who told us about this guy," I retorted. "If you didn't want us to go after him, you shouldn't have given us his picture."

Agent Bergerschmidt opened her mouth to deliver a no-doubt stern rebuke to that, but a ruckus at the door of Tanzarian's mansion interrupted her.

"Let me through, you Stormtrooper, my kids are in there!"

A bulky Homeland Security agent was shoved back against the wall. A petite curly-haired woman nearly half his size pushed past him. It was Brynn, and my dad was right behind her. My stepmom rushed down the hallway, wrapping me and Val in a suffocating mama-bear hug.

"What are you—how could you have—thank God you're all right!" she said in a single breath, then pulled back to inspect our faces. "*Are* you all right?"

"We're fine," I said, still a bit strangled from the hug. "Val might be a bit hungry."

"Ma ma ma," agreed the baby, reaching for Brynn.

"Robbie," my dad began, struggling to find his words. "How could you—stealing your sister—and to the home of a *criminal*—"

"I'm sorry," I said quickly. "But I swear, we did this to protect Val. We wanted to find out who did this to her, and why they're targeting—"

He cut me off: "You did this for yourself, Robbie. You think you're a superhero? You are thirteen *years old*! You're not a hero, you're not a law enforcement agent, and you are certainly not acting like her brother. Not if you're breaking into mansions and dangling her in front of attack dogs!"

Fletcher raised an ill-advised finger. "Actually, Tanzarian brought the dog to—"

"And you!" said my dad, rounding on my best friend. "I don't know where your parents are in all this, but you have been far too much of a bad influence on my son. But that? Is over. No more sleepovers, no more hanging out, no communication of any kind with the outside world. As of this moment, Robbie, and for the rest of the summer, you are *grounded.*"

Our drive home to Pasadena was quiet. I wasn't worried, though—my dad had "grounded" me once or twice before. With a laptop, iPad, and PlayStation at my disposal, being confined to the house wasn't exactly a horrible prospect. In fact, before my sister had started bouncing around the room, it was how I had planned to spend most of my summer vacation anyway.

But I wasn't prepared for how upset my dad was. The second we got home, he started unplugging electronic devices and dropping them in a large cardboard box. After that he gathered up all my comic books and threw those in as well. Then went my various posters and superhero-themed artwork. By the end of it, my room was more empty than a prison cell in Puritan Massachusetts.

"You can't just take all my stuff away!" I said as he locked up the huge box in the garage. "I'm a human being—I have rights!"

"And what about your sister's rights?" my dad shot back, cinching a combination lock on the garage door. Brynn watched us from the driveway, cuddling Val to her. "She hasn't had a say in any of this. She didn't decide to go rescue drowning people or fight hostage takers—you did that. You and your morally bankrupt, comic-book-crazed buddy. What you two did to her was a *crime*, Robbie. And it could have ended in your deaths any number of times. But today? Today you crossed a line. Now hand me your phone."

I had never seen him this angry. I didn't hesitate in taking out my iPhone and handing it over. "You're gonna leave me without a phone, too?" I said, trying to sound defiant. "I thought you got that for me in case of emergencies."

"Oh, you'll still be able to use it for that," he said, thumbing in access codes. One of the conditions of me getting a phone was that he knew all my passcodes. He held down the power button, then handed the phone back to me. "Only now, that's all you'll be able to use it for."

I looked down at the iPhone screen. A small window informed me that a factory reset was in progress. My dad had erased everything I had. All my Superkid research, our crime-fighting photos, my games—gone. I was so mad, it took me a moment to form words. "You . . . Why . . . You can't do that!"

"Now you know what it feels like," he said, "to have something you care about taken from you without permission."

He walked back into the house. I jogged after him. "What am I supposed to for the rest of the summer? You want me to think about what I did? I already have, okay, and I'm sorry. What else do you want me to say?"

He pulled a thick leather-bound brick of a book off a shelf and tossed it to me. Stamped on the cover in gold lettering were the words *California Penal Code*. "You can start by reading that. Make a list of every law you broke, using your sister like you did. Now go to your room."

* * *

The next nine days were horrible. From sunrise to sundown, I had to stay in my room. I was allowed to leave for meals and bathroom breaks, but that was it. My dad and Brynn hired a new nanny to watch Val and (I suspected) to keep an eye on me. Her name was Hildy, and she wasn't a spacey pushover like Shelby had been. Hildy was a fifty-three-year-old East German immigrant who had lived under Communist rule for twenty years before coming to the States. Even though she'd been here for thirty-plus years and the Cold War had ended long ago, she still acted like she was fighting Commies on the daily. And in this case, I was Mother Russia.

I quickly realized there would be no scamming Hildy. She watched me every second I was out of my room, and she did random room checks throughout the day. Fletcher showed up at my bedroom window once, but Hildy caught him and kicked him off the property.

I was completely cut off from the world. My dad had blocked all my friends' numbers on our phones, and he'd put a parental lock on all the electronics to prevent me from downloading any apps. I had no idea what people were saying about Superkid, if they were saying anything at all. I couldn't check my email or watch TV or even go on Twitter.

What I could do was read. I flipped through the *California Penal Code* for a bit, but my eyes started to cross after a couple lines. I tossed the thick book aside and went back to the fantasy novels I'd loved as a kid—The Chronicles of Narnia, *The Lord of the Rings*, The Dark Is Rising Sequence, the Abhorsen trilogy. They gave me a break from the crushing boredom of my empty room. But they also were a painful reminder that, for a handful of weeks, I had been the center of my own fantastic adventure.

Now that adventure was over. I was locked up, and my parents had begun researching how to put Val's powers on lockdown as well. They spoke with several doctors about suppressing her abilities through hypnotism or reinforcement training. They even debated putting the now eleven-month-old baby on tranquilizers. Thankfully, my sister hadn't done anything in the last week and a half to encourage that behavior. In fact, the only time she cranked up her EM field was when she was around me. Clearly, she'd come to think of our crime fighting as some sort of game, but my dad and Brynn were not amused. They made sure that Val and I were never alone together.

I began to resign myself to my fate. My parents would soon figure out how to neutralize Val's superpowers, and then any chance I had of doing something awesome would be gone. I'd go back to being Boring, Ordinary Robbie.

Then, at five a.m. on the tenth day of my confinement, something extraordinary happened.

"The Imperial March" from *Star Wars* startled me awake. I'd chosen the ringtone to designate any unknown number. I didn't know anyone who would call so early in the morning, but I answered it anyway. At that point, any break in my monotonous routine was welcome. "Hello?"

"Robbie, it's Fletch. I'm on a burner phone."

"Fletcher? What's wrong?"

"It's time to wake up, dude. Get Val, get your parents, and get the eff outta Dodge."

"It's five in the morning."

"Which is why you have to leave now. She could be there any second."

I got up, peeking out at the street. It was still dark at this hour, and empty. "Who?"

"Bergerface. She's the Phoenix."

I groaned. "We've been over this. Just 'cause she works for the government, doesn't mean—"

"Guess where she worked before Homeland: military research, dude. DARPA let her go, almost everything's redacted, but my dad's PI pulled a file from the last case she was on there. The suspect? Armin Tanzarian."

"So what?"

"So—word around DARPA is, Bacon Berger went to the Dark Side. She wanted to buy Fortis for the military so they could make their very own super soldiers. Tanzarian got to the meteorite first."

I turned on my bedroom light, fully awake now. "Your dad's investigator found all this?"

"I told you, he's good. Plus, my dad's lawyer wanted to have some evidence locked and loaded in case this turned into a legal action. He told us that Bergertime? Hasn't logged a single file from the Tanzarian bust. The meteorite your sister nearly gave up her toes for, it's gone."

I pulled on a T-shirt and shorts. "Why are you telling me this now?"

"Because, the PI put a tracker on Bergerbarf's car, and she's headed your way."

I checked the street again. Still dark and empty. "Are you sure?"

"Dude, she came after us, too. I've been hiding out in a motel for two days with Yegor. You wouldn't believe the crappy TV I've had to watch. If you don't wanna end up in some CIA black site, you guys need to leave. Now."

As I watched the street, a white government-issue van and a fussy Ford Taurus pulled up across the way. I quickly turned off my light, seeing Bergerschmidt step out of the Taurus. "Oh my God, you're right. She's here."

"Don't answer the door, do not answer your phone. In fact, ditch the phone altogether. Don't use credit cards, email, or anything else that can track you. I'll contact you at Stark Tower tomorrow. May the Force be with you."

"But, but . . ."

But Fletcher hung up. I was left to face a team of federal agents all by myself.

Calm down, I told myself. *You're not entirely alone*. I went into my parents' room. I knew turning on their light might alert the Feds, so I cleared my throat. "Wake up, guys. It's an emergency."

My dad continued to snore, but Brynn rolled over. "Objection, Your Honor," she muttered in a sleepy voice.

I rolled my eyes, then walked over and jostled my dad's shoulder. "Wake up," I whispered.

He sat up immediately, his eyes wide. "Robbie? What's wrong?"

"We have to go. Get Brynn up and pack some clothes. I'll go get Val." I crossed the hall into my sister's room. She stirred as I lifted her from the crib, making a few pathetic fussy sounds before putting her adorable little head back on my shoulder and closing her eyes.

I returned to my parents' room. Both Brynn and my dad were now awake and getting dressed. They had turned the light on, so I shut it off. My dad was peeved. "Robbie, if this is some kind of prank—"

"It's not. Bergerschmidt's outside with a whole van full of agents, and she wants to take Val away from us." I passed my sister over to

Brynn. My dad went to the window, and I followed. Outside, Bergerschmidt was giving directions to five government-suited agents. Three of them nodded, then began to fan out around our house. Each one held a pistol.

My dad's anger began to fade. "Why . . . why wouldn't she call us?"

"Because she's the bad guy," I told him. "She already stole the meteorite, and she tried to take out Fletcher, too. Now, you guys pack and grab as much money as you can. Val and I will hold them off."

I reached for my sister, but Brynn backed away. "Robbie, I don't think . . . Your dad and I talked about this, and . . ." She looked to him for help.

"We don't want Val using her powers anymore," he said. "At least, not until she can choose to do so on her own."

Unbelievable. These two had given birth to Supergirl, but they wanted to keep her in a kryptonite diaper. "Fine, I'll do it myself. Do *not* turn on your cell phones."

"Wait," said my dad. "What are you going to do?"

"Don't worry," I grinned. "I'm just gonna introduce Bergerschmidt to a little movie called *Home Alone.*"

"Which one?" my dad whispered after me. "Robbie, wait!" But I was already making my way down the stairs.

The first time I saw *Home Alone*, I did what a lot of nine-year-olds do: I drafted my own overly complicated blueprints for home defense. I hadn't thought about them in years, but the most obvious points of entry were still valid. And thanks to my baby sister, I had plenty of materials for traps.

When I reached the downstairs living room, I could already see the silhouettes of two agents skulking through the backyard. Keeping myself low, I silently scooted Val's jungle seat under the back dining room window. Then I picked up one of my sister's least favorite stuffed animals, a purple alligator, and sped into the kitchen. I pulled a steak knife out of the wooden block and slit the alligator's belly. Millions of tiny beads spread across the tile, forming a large puddle in front of the garage door.

I doubled back to the pantry, pulling out an armload of Val's squeezy pouches. My dad called these "baby MREs," since they were basically whizzed-up meal substitutes in a bag. They were all pretty gross, but they'd make a solid intruder countermeasure.

I unscrewed the caps of the pouches, then squeezed the goopy gray-brown contents all over the floor in front of the back patio door. I tried to resist gagging at the smell. A glance outside told me the agents were only a few feet away. It was time to blow this Popsicle stand. I tiptoed back toward the staircase, nearly jumping out my skin when the doorbell rang.

I held my breath. My heart pounded like a bongo drum played by a dude who'd had too many Red Bulls. A knock came next—*rap rap rap rap rap.*

"Mr. Rampino? Mrs. Cooper-Rampino? It's Agent Bergerschmidt. We need to chat, STAT. And yes, I am aware that rhymes."

Slowly, I inched myself toward the peephole. The Homeland Security agent stood on our front porch, her Sig Sauer in hand. She looked as sour and brusque as ever. Behind her was another, bulkier Homeland agent, with a heavy metal door ram in his hands.

"Crap," I whispered.

Bergerschmidt suddenly leaned forward, her stern face only a few inches from mine. "Robbie? If that's you, open the door."

Slowly, I backed away from the door—

And stepped on Val's rubber giraffe. It gave a high-pitched, cartoony *squeak-squeeee.* Double crap.

On the front porch, Bergerschmidt pressed a finger to her earpiece. "They know we're here. Breach, breach."

A window was smashed open in the dining room. I spun to see a

Homeland agent lift up the transom, climb through the opening . . .

And step right into the jungle seat. Colored lights flashed, and annoying animal sounds played a top volume. The agent's foot became tangled in the fabric leg hole, pulling her to the floor. One down.

Next came a *smash* from the kitchen patio door. A second agent reached through the broken pane and unlocked the dead bolt, but he wasn't expecting a squeezy pouch puddle at his feet. The moment his dress shoe touched the slick spot of baby slurm, it went out from under him. He fell hard on the tile floor, his pistol skittering across the kitchen.

I heard, but didn't see, another agent enter through the door to the garage. There was a skittering of beads, a muffled curse, then a very heavy-sounding *thump*. A gun went off, sending a bullet up through the ceiling and punching a hole in my dad's bed pillow. Thankfully, neither he nor Brynn nor Val were anywhere near it at the time.

The sound finally sent my legs into action. They carried me toward the staircase. Just as I reached the bottom, a metal ram knocked our front door off its hinges. It fell inward, the open doorway backlighting Bergerschmidt like the Big Bad from a horror movie.

"Don't make this difficult, Robbie," she said.

In response, I kicked over Val's toy chest. Bristle blocks, teething toys, and a zoo's worth of large plastic animals spilled over the ground between us. It might not stop her, but it would definitely slow her down.

Bergerschmidt sighed. "See, that? Is being difficult." She motioned the other Homeland agent forward, and they began picking their way through the infant mine field.

I ran upstairs. I hopped over the baby gate at the top, ducked into my parents' room, closed the doors, and cinched a plastic child lock over the knobs.

"Are you okay? I think they shot our bed!" said Brynn. My parents were freaked, but at least they'd managed to get dressed and pack some things while I was downstairs. Val was awake and in her baby carrier on my dad's chest. She clapped at me sleepily.

"I told you, she's the bad guy," I said. "You guys have everything you need? Cash? Diapers? Passports?"

"Passports?" sputtered my dad. "Look, Robbie—these people are federal agents. Maybe we can talk to them, or—"

The bedroom doorknob rattled. "Mr. Rampino? Mrs. Cooper-Rampino? It's Agent Bergerschmidt. I apologize for the hour, but we need you to come with us. Now."

"You see?" I whispered. "Would a good guy show up in the middle of the night and break down our door? If she takes us in, they will never let us go. Especially Val."

Brynn bit her lip. "He has a point, Mike. If the government wanted, they could charge us as enemy combatants. They could hold us indefinitely."

"Whatever Robbie's telling you, he's incorrect," said Bergerschmidt through the door. "We want to protect you."

"Oh yeah? Then why'd you shoot a bullet through my parents' bed?" I asked her. I lowered my voice and turned back to my parents. "You know we can't trust the government. We have to go on the run, at least until we figure out what's going on."

Brynn and I turned to my dad. He was a college film professor, not a fighter. He'd never been arrested, or even gotten so much as a speeding ticket. He paid his taxes on time, reported for jury duty, and voted in every election. He'd never expected to be a fugitive.

But now he nodded. "How do we get away?"

"I've got an idea," I told him.

As I outlined my plan, Bergerschmidt grew tired of waiting. "Back away from the door, please. We're coming in." She aimed her pistol, firing three quick, efficient bullets. Two punched through the respective doorknobs and the third cut through the plastic child lock. There was a low *thrum* as she pushed open the door.

But my parents' bedroom was empty.

Bergerschmidt and the other agents checked the bathroom, the walk-in closet, even under the bed. Nothing. She stepped on to the small back balcony. A quick scan told her we weren't in the yard below, either. Had she looked a little farther off, she would have seen a clump of people-shaped shadows float behind a magnolia tree a block away.

Instead she went back inside. My parents and I touched down on the street, having clung to the baby carrier while Val repelled her way down the block. I shook out my sore arms.

"That's a lot easier when she's attached to your chest," I complained.

"What do we do now?" Brynn whispered. "We can't take our car—they'll spot us."

My dad was already requesting a ride from Lyft on his phone. "We cut through these yards, and a car will pick us up on Orange Grove in . . . five minutes."

As we hustled through the dewy side yards of darkened houses, I tried to find a silver lining in this turn of events. By the time we reached Orange Grove Boulevard, I had it.

"There's one good thing that came out of this," I told them as our Lyft driver pulled up in a silver Chevy Suburban. "At least I'm no longer grounded."

I may have been freed from my bedroom prison, but I soon realized that my parents and I had entered a new kind of oppressive environment. Forget what you've seen in movies and TV shows. I can tell you from personal experience that being on the run sucks. Imagine freaking out every time you see a law enforcement official. Or using only cash to buy everything you need. Or worrying about being caught on camera any time you step outside. A few hours into my time as a government fugitive, I realized I had less freedom than when my dad had put me under house arrest.

Thankfully, our Lyft driver managed to get us to Union Station in downtown Los Angeles without any interference from Bergerschmidt or Homeland Security. From there we bought train tickets to Bakersfield, carving a big hunk out of my dad's wad of cash. We pulled into the scruffy town around lunchtime and my dad booked a room in a cheap motel using more of our money. Double-Doubles and Animal Style fries from In-N-Out dwindled our financial situation even further.

Now we were all sitting around the motel room, which was gritty in every sense of the word, and debating what to do next. My dad and Brynn only had about a hundred dollars left in their pile o' cash, and none of us had a plan. Brynn was changing Val, who had been unusually fussy all day. My dad was flipping through TV channels, and I was surfing the Web on the family iPad. We were the top story on every news site and channel.

"Shocking developments in the ongoing saga of Superkid," said a BBC news anchor on the TV. "According to sources in the United States Department of Homeland Security, the world's first superhero has been kidnapped."

My dad clicked to the next channel, a feed from an Indian news channel. A female anchor was also covering us. "The infant and her handler have supposedly been abducted by this couple," she said as pictures of Brynn and my dad appeared next to her head.

My dad clicked again, this time to a Japanese news anchor. We couldn't understand what he was saying, but thankfully there were subtitles: *Film professor Michael Rampino and entertainment lawyer Brynn Cooper-Rampino. All involved are in serious danger, and we urge our audience—*"

My dad flipped again. This time it was our old buddy Fran Caulder. She was well into one of her patented "all sass, no facts" rants. "These criminals have abducted, used, and abused a poor lil' child of Christ. They have made her a lightning rod for sin and danger. I urge my devoted fans, if y'all see these child-stealing monsters, for the love of G-dash-d, call the Amber Alert folks here." A hotline number appeared onscreen, but my dad couldn't take any more. He shut off the TV and put his head in his hands.

Brynn lifted Val off the bed, bouncing the crying baby against her chest in an attempt to soothe her. "I gotta hand it to Bergerschmidt. Casting us as baby-nappers makes it much more likely that people will call it in. We'll have to start wearing disguises." I guessed that her lawyering experience had prepared her for situations like this, because she sounded oddly calm.

"I told you, she's an evil genius," I said. "If she's the one who switched your prenatal vitamins, she's been planning this for almost two years."

My dad was way less chill than Brynn and I. "*If* she did it? *If*? Why did she even pick us in the first place? This whole thing is insane. We're fugitives! From the law. Look at how upset Val is."

My baby sister wailed even louder. Brynn tried to give her a bottle of formula, but the eleven-month-old shook her head, turning away.

My dad began pacing the room. It was something he always did when he was really agitated. "Maybe . . . I don't know, maybe we should turn ourselves in. Tell the police everything. At least the kids'll be safe."

"No way," I said. "They've already decided we're guilty. We'll be sent to some offshore interrogation prison."

"What do you want us to do, then? Find some cabin in the Alaskan wilderness? Hide out forever?" He increased his pacing. "I can't even build a fire without a starter log."

"We will need some way of making money," Brynn agreed. "Homeland Security has probably frozen all our bank accounts by now."

"And that's just survival," my dad continued. "What about our jobs? What about school? You two want to spend the rest of your lives wandering from town to town?"

"Oooh, like Bruce Banner in *The Incredible Hulk*," Brynn said excitedly. Then, seeing the appalled look on my dad's face: "Sorry, I loved that show as a kid. But it's probably not a realistic life plan these days."

My dad shook his head. "We're not cut out for this. We're

parents—regular, middle-class, suburban parents. Not globe-trotting vigilantes."

"Speak for yourself," I said, flipping around the iPad to show a transaction page on Craigslist. "I found a dude right here in Bakersfield willing to swap his car for our iPads and an iPhone. Boom."

My dad peered at the overweight, tank-top-wearing dude's sketchy picture. "Well, he looks very trustworthy."

"You go on the run, this is the class of person you gotta work with," I said, trying to sound more knowledgeable than I really was. "Once we have some wheels, we can meet up with Fletcher and figure out a plan. He might even be able to loan us some money. His dad's got cash stashed all over the place. He doesn't trust banks."

"And how do you plan to contact Fletcher?" said my dad. "You send anything from our email accounts, and Bergerschmidt will be able to trace the IP addresses."

Fletcher had already thought of a solution to this problem when he'd called me at five in the morning. I couldn't believe that was less than twelve hours ago. "We can talk through Stark Tower. It's an online comic book forum. All the users are anonymous, so it should be a while until Bergerschmidt figures out it's us."

Val wailed again. For the first time ever, food didn't seem to be calming her. Maybe she could sense how stressed we were. "Won't she be watching the site, though?" asked Brynn. "I would if I were her."

"Stepmom, please," I said. "All the comics I've read, you think I can't come up with a way to send a secret message?"

* * *

We met the sketchy Craigslist dude in a Del Taco parking lot, swapping our freshly reset Apple products for his beat-up Ford Fiesta. (I made sure to have my dad give up his phone instead of mine.) The Fiesta's engine made a squealing noise upon starting and it had more dings than the distance markers at a driving range, but at least we were freed from the cash-draining prospect of public transportation.

We swung through a drugstore to stock up on disguise hats, sunglasses, and baby supplies, then crowded around a computer at the local public library. Even though our conversation would be anonymous, it was possible Bergerschmidt had listened to this morning's phone call. If she did figure out what Stark Tower was, and had traced the IP addresses of the users to their point of origin, then all she would know was that we'd been through Bakersfield.

Val's fussing had continued throughout the afternoon, and no attempt to soothe her had worked. "I think she's sick," Brynn said as I logged in to the Stark Tower forum. "We've fed her, changed her diaper, tried to give her a nap—why else would she be so cranky? Does she feel warm to you?"

My dad placed a hand on the baby's forehead. She moaned pathetically. "Maybe. I don't know. It's summer in Bakersfield; we're all warm."

"Maybe you should take her outside," I whispered, seeing an older woman glare in our direction. "It'll suck if her nonstop crying is what gets us caught."

Val sneezed. There was a sudden *thrum* as she sent out an EM burst, making several computers in the next row crackle with electricity. The old woman yelped.

"That was weird," I said loudly, looking around in suspicion. "These computers must be pretty old." I bent behind my monitor, whispering fiercely. "Will one of you take her out of here, please?"

Brynn hoisted the baby on her hip and started out of the computer lab. My sister sneezed again, making four computers crackle and causing a metal fire extinguisher to fall off the wall. "Cheap government equipment," I said for the benefit of the room. "I, for one, plan to fill out a strongly worded comment card!"

"Tone it down," whispered my dad. He pointed to a discussion tab I'd created called *All-American Comics*. "What's that?"

"The name of the comic line that featured the debut of our favorite superhero," I said. "Green Lantern."

My dad blinked, confused. "I thought you hated that guy."

"The movie version, yes," I said. "But the comics are great. Especially the villains. Like Sinestro? See, he was a good guy at first, actually trained Hal Jordan—"

My dad cut me off. "We're on the run for our lives. Just a reminder."

"Right. Well, all Fletch has to do is type in Sinestro's homeworld, and we can have a private chat session." I hit the return key and sat back, satisfied with my clever hacking skills.

"So that's it?" my dad said. "How long do we have to sit here until—"

Ding. A notification appeared on my computer screen: *User Darth_Derth has joined your conversation!*

"You see?" I said. "There he is."

A chat message appeared onscreen: *DOOD, nice work with the Lantern refs. Where r u?*

"Best keep it vague, in case Bergerschmidt finds this," my dad advised.

I nodded, my fingers already tapping at the keyboard: *Somewhere safe and dry, for the mo. What do we do?*

Gotta meet up. Six heads > one.

Agreed, I typed. *Where r U??*

A couple hours outside Coast City.

"Coast City?" asked my dad.

"Green Lantern's hometown," I explained. "It's, like, the DC version of Los Angeles or San Diego."

"Good, so he's still close by."

"I hope so." I typed a response: *Us 2. Meetup place suggestions?*

There was a pause, then Fletcher's answer appeared: *Where Scott Lang met Godzilla.*

My dad rolled his eyes. "Okay, I take it back. The comic book code is making me nuts. Where is that?"

"I don't know," I admitted. "But Scott Lang is Ant-Man, and Godzilla—"

"—is a giant, irradiated lizard," my dad said huffily. "I am a film professor, remember? But as far as I know, those two were never in a movie together."

"They weren't. Godzilla's from Japan, and Ant-Man . . . That's it." I opened a new browser window and pulled up a Google map of . . .

"San Francisco?" said my dad.

"Both movies, the recent ones, were set there," I explained. "Fletch even had a whole rant about how the city's too overused as a movie backdrop. He said just once, he'd like to see something set in St. Paul, or Akron, or—"

"On the run. Lives," my dad reminded me.

"Okay, okay. How about this place?" I zoomed in on the map, pointing to a spot in the middle of a huge San Francisco park.

"The Legion of Honor?" said my dad. "It's public, plenty of open space . . . That should work."

Okay, I typed. *The kaiju will find Legions of Honor 2morrow at 5 p.m.*

NICE, Fletcher responded. *C U there.*

I closed the chat window and checked the route on Google maps. "It's about three hundred miles. Five hours or so with traffic. If we leave early in the morning, we should get there with plenty of—" A loud *thrum* outside the library interrupted me. An EM burst shook the computer room, making the screens flicker. A spiderweb of cracks appeared in the window. Brynn frantically signaled us from outside.

Val was in her arms, red-faced and struggling. We couldn't hear them, but my baby sister's discomfort was obvious.

"I think your stepmom's right," my dad said. "We better stop by the drugstore again and get some baby medicine."

"Good idea," I said, then raised my voice. "It's impossible to use these janky computers anyway. Am I right?" I asked the old lady. She sourly pursed her mouth and looked away. You can't win with some people.

"Still too much," said my dad as we exited the computer room.

Sick babies are a hassle even at the best of times. They feel crappy, but they can't tell you why they feel crappy, so there's a lot of tears involved on both sides. But when you take a sick baby, give her electromagnetic superpowers, put her inside a busted-up Ford Fiesta, then attempt to drive that car to San Francisco without drawing the attention of the authorities—well, let's just say *crappy* doesn't begin to cover it.

My whole family was exhausted. Val's fussing and occasional sneeze/EM blasts had kept everyone from sleeping the night before. We'd gotten up at seven a.m. to pack, eaten a greasy fast-food breakfast, and were now heading north on the 5. The drive had been harrowing. Val kept wailing in the back seat, while Brynn tried to soothe her from the other rear seat. I was counting down the miles from the front passenger seat, and my frazzled dad was behind the wheel.

Val sneezed, sending another EM blast through the car. Sparks crackled off the metal frame, the side windows cracked, and the cloth headrest of my seat caught on fire. I calmly aimed the fire extinguisher we'd taken from our motel room, and gave a short pull on the handle. A small burst of white foam put out the flames, leaving behind a damp black scorch mark. There were about a half dozen similar marks all over the car.

"Bless you," Brynn said, wiping Val's itty-bitty nose.

"Good thing we didn't pay much for this junker," I added.

Val sneezed again, this time making a hubcap pop off and the metal roof buckle. The Fiesta swerved, but my dad managed to stay in our lane.

"We should have swapped for a tank," he said grimly.

"Bless you," Brynn said again, rubbing the baby's back.

"Ow-ahh, mama," said Val, sticking out her lower lip in the cutest display of discomfort possible.

"Should I give her more ibuprofen?" Brynn asked. "It hasn't quite been six hours, but maybe it will help her sleep."

"Give her anything that will get us to San Francisco without dying," suggested my dad.

Brynn fished through her purse, which was no small feat itself. My stepmom wasn't messy, but she carried a lot of random items with her, in case they might be needed. Today she pulled out a wad of unopened Band-Aids, a linty pacifier, a package of crushed oyster crackers, and a small tape measure before locating the ibuprofen.

She filled the dropper and tried to place it in Val's tiny mouth, but the baby resisted. One, two, then three EM blasts shook the car. The back window blew out. The passenger door buckled. Sparks spewed from the radio. But Brynn kept her hand firmly on her daughter's head until the baby gave up. She squirted the bubble-gum-flavored medicine into Val's mouth and rubbed her throat until she swallowed.

"Burbee blow bah," Val said in annoyance.

"There we go," said Brynn. "Not that much farther, hon."

"Speak for yourself," said my dad as we passed a green freeway sign that read SAN FRANCISCO—185 MILES. It was gonna be a long drive.

* * *

A little over five hours later, a block of battered, smoking metal that used to be our Ford Fiesta shuddered to a stop in front of the Legion of Honor museum. The building was made of white stone, carved into Roman-style columns. A thirty-foot-high central archway led to an open-air courtyard. In the center of the courtyard was a bronze sculpture of a large naked dude sitting on the toilet. I knew this famous work of art was called *The Thinker*, but come on—we all know what he's really doing.

My dad let go of the steering wheel for the first time in hours and turned off the car. He flexed his stiff fingers and tried to flatten down his frizzy EM-blasted hair. After a morning of fighting against Val's inadvertent superpower outbursts, we all looked pretty messed up. Our clothes were scorched, our skin was bruised, and each of us looked like our hair had been styled by the Bride of Frankenstein.

"Well, that wasn't so bad," whispered Brynn. Val had finally fallen asleep about fifteen minutes ago, and none of us had spoken above a murmur for fear of waking her.

Both my dad and I closed our eyes. It was the only way we could prevent ourselves from screaming at her in frustration.

"Tell you what," my stepmom continued. "How about I go find Fletcher? You two stay here and rest."

We nodded, too exhausted to form words. Brynn leaned forward, giving each of us a kiss on the head. She touched the driver's-side passenger door, and it fell off its hinges, hitting the ground with a massive *clunk*. Val stirred, but thankfully slept on.

"We'll fix that when I get back," said Brynn. Gingerly, she stepped over the car door and made her way toward the museum. The grounds were filled with tourists, local residents on their lunch break, and the occasional street performer. My dad and I watched Brynn enter the courtyard and walk past *The Crapper*, then we leaned back and closed our eyes again.

It was only a few seconds later that a scream broke the quiet.

Brynn's scream.

My dad and I bolted upright, scanning the crowd. There was no sign of my stepmom. No sign of any disturbance at all—

And then she ran past a column. A huge, muscled man in a black tee, black camo pants, and a black ski mask tore after her, wrapping a thick arm around her waist. His other hand clapped over her mouth. Brynn kicked, trying to pull herself free, but it was like fighting against a sequoia tree. She bit down on the man's gloved finger, freeing her mouth enough to yell:

"Robbie! Michael! Protect Val!"

Then Sequoia Man dragged her out of sight. Instinctively, my dad got out of the car, but stopped when he saw another mercenary striding toward us. He, too, was in black military clothes and wore a black ski mask over his face. As he drew closer, I could see a white bird had been stitched into the thick black wool. A phoenix. I could also see that his pupils were the size of quarters, and they were vibrating. He'd been exposed to Fortis.

"Dad . . ." I said warningly. I knew he was torn between going after Brynn and staying with us.

Then the mercenary took a MAC-10 Uzi from his jacket, and my dad's mind was made up. He got back into the Fiesta and tried to turn on the car, but the keys fell from his fingers. I bent down to get them. When I sat back up, the mercenary's ski-mask-covered face was filling my window.

"Cute kid," he said in a creepy, calm voice, then smashed his forehead through my window. Tiny cubes of safety glass bounced off my face and shoulders. I swung the fire extinguisher into the mercenary's face. There was a deep, heavy *bong* as it connected with his skull, but the guy didn't even move. Only his pupils continued to vibrate like two angry hornets.

While I was in a stare-down with Creepy Calmy, my dad had managed to wrangle the car key into the ignition. He turned them now, and the engine coughed itself to life. He put the car into drive and hit the gas.

The Ford Fiesta leapt forward. Rather than be left behind, Creepy Calmly latched a hand onto my doorframe and let himself be dragged down the street. His other hand shot forward, wrapping around my windpipe. He squeezed.

"Dad," I managed to choke out. "Veer . . . right!"

My dad glanced over and saw what I was dealing with. He veered the Fiesta toward a parked station wagon. I fumbled to open my door—

And Creepy Calmy slammed into the back of the vehicle, popping off our car and releasing my throat. My door swung shut, now free of mercenaries.

"Ha!" I said, turning to gloat at my attacker. "Don't let the door hit you on the way—"

But my zinger died before I could complete it. Creepy Calmy stood, barely bruised from his run-in with the parked car.

"Seriously?" I said.

A windowless white van careened around the corner. It slowed next to Creepy Calmy and he hopped into the front passenger seat, never once taking his eyes off us. The van's driver hit the gas, gunning straight for us.

"Bad news," I said to my dad. "Now we gotta take part in a car chase."

"I only teach action movies," he complained. "I wasn't built to *be* in one."

He accelerated onto El Camino Del Mar. As the Fiesta crossed over Lobos Creek, the street became Lincoln Boulevard. The gorgeous two-lane highway was framed by the Pacific Ocean on one side and a forested, former army base called the Presidio on the other. If we had to be pursued by a bunch of drug-riddled psychos, at least it was happening against a pretty backdrop.

Since it was a weekday, the traffic wasn't too congested. My dad managed to get around a couple of slower cars, but with my baby sister asleep in the back seat and the Fiesta's decrepit engine, we weren't exactly putting out an Indy 500 vibe.

The white van had no such issues. The guy behind the wheel had the benefit of military experience, as well as a complete disregard for other drivers. Our pursuers swerved in and out of their lane, cutting around cars and scaring oncoming vehicles off the road. Even though we'd had a good lead coming into Lincoln Boulevard, within minutes the mercenaries were right behind us. Their car shot forward.

"Don't do it!" I yelled at them.

CRUNCH. They rammed the back of the Fiesta. Our rear bumper fell off, making the white van's driver hit the brakes and swerve to avoid it.

"Hey, baby on board, a-holes!" I shouted.

Whether it was my shouting or the car-rattling impact, Val woke up and started to cry. I reached back to put her pacifier in her mouth. She looked up at me, her innocent eyes questioning. "Don't worry," I said to her. "We're gonna get you out of this."

I slid back into the front seat and buckled my seat belt. "I'm not lying, am I?" I said to my dad.

"Well, we can't outrun them," he replied. "But maybe we can lose them. Hold on, kids."

He cut the steering wheel hard to the right, turning on to Kobbe Avenue. We were now driving through the forest, directly toward the

Presidio. The white van shot past us, hitting its brakes and making a U-turn.

My dad turned down another street. We found ourselves in a parking lot surrounded by white military-style buildings. The Fiesta sped through the tight rows, causing a few people to jump out of the way.

"Sorry!" he yelled, laying on the horn. "Never drive like this, Robbie."

We reached the end of the lot, and he drove right over the curb. There was a massive bump, then we were speeding across a manicured lawn.

"Just out of curiosity, do you know where we're going?" I asked.

"Not yet. But I'm working on it."

He cut the wheel again, jumping the curb and landing us another paved road. This one twisted even deeper into the woods. We seemed to have lost the white van . . .

Until it tore out of a side street, just barely missing us. The driver swerved, but kept coming at us.

"Come on!" complained my dad. "They must be using GPS. That's not fair."

"It's a car chase, Dad. I don't think 'fair' enters into it."

The white van pulled alongside us. Creepy Calmy gave us a smile and a pleasant wave from the passenger seat.

Then they plowed right into us.

WHAM! The van crunched into the side of our car. The Fiesta spun around, but my dad managed to keep the clunker on the road. Val sneezed, making the dashboard spark with a minor EM blast.

"Bless you," I said absently. "Actually . . . hit the brakes!"

My dad did so. While our car squealed to a stop, the white van shot across the road, completely missing a second chance to sideswipe the Fiesta.

I unbuckled my seat belt, climbing into the back. "Okay, baby girl," I said to my sister. "Ready to get those sniffles out?"

"What are you doing?" asked my dad. "They're backing up."

"Good, pull alongside them," I said.

"As someone who's been driving for twenty-five years, I try to avoid getting in the blind spot of psychos!"

"Well, I'm the one with the superhero experience. Trust me."

My dad shook his head, but accelerated toward the van full of mercenaries. I climbed into the back seat, unhooking one of Val's car seat latches. "Don't let us down now, baby girl," I breathed, angling her toward the white van. I waited until I could see the vibrating pupils of Creepy Calmy's eyes, then:

"Bless you!" I shouted. My sister reacted in surprise, but two days of repetition had done its work. Val sneezed, sending a massive EM burst through the open doorless hole in our car, and directly into the cab of the white van. Sparks crackled off the vehicle's dashboard, shorting out the electricity and making the engine stall. The white van swung wildly across the road. The driver pumped the brakes, but they were temporarily out. The car went off the road and plowed into a pine tree. There it stayed.

"Yes!" I whooped. "That's not a gesundheit—it's a 'got done right.'"

"Cut the quips," said my dad. "And no more weaponizing your sister."

"Are you kidding? She just saved our butts."

"And what if she does that to someone who's not a mercenary? If she can't control her powers, it's better that she doesn't use them at—"

PING! BONG! Two metallic noises from the rear of the car cut him off. We both looked back. Creepy Calmy had leapt from the white van and was sprinting down the street after us. In his hand was the MAC-10 Uzi. The noises we'd heard had been bullets striking the Ford Fiesta.

"Duck!" shouted my dad, stepping on the gas again. The Fiesta growled, but didn't exactly spring forward. Creepy Calmy pulled the trigger of his gun again. More bullets ricocheted off the trunk of the car, but one found a different target.

BOOSH. One of our rear tires blew out, making the car fishtail. There was a *FLAPFLAPFLAP* as torn rubber spun around the wheel well. My dad turned around a corner, but our long-distance driving plans were effectively shredded. The time had come to ditch the Fiesta.

Up ahead, I could see the red towers of the Golden Gate Bridge rising above the treetops. They shone like a beacon in the late-afternoon sun. "Can you get us to the bridge?" I asked.

My dad had seen it too. "Maybe," he said. "But it won't be fast or pretty. What do you have in mind now?"

"I don't know," I admitted. "But hopefully there will be enough people there that we can lose these guys."

We took a few more turns, ending up on Lincoln Boulevard again. The car was only going about twenty miles an hour now. Sparks sprayed from the wheel well and the Fiesta pulled strongly to the left, but we made it out of the Presidio. The battered, hobbled car coasted downhill toward the bridge, the west opening of which was clogged with traffic and tourists. Once we got there, we could ditch the car, blend in with the crowds, and lose the mercenaries. Or so I hoped.

"Shoot," said my dad suddenly. He pumped the brakes, but nothing happened. "Shoot, shoot, shoot. Uh, the brakes are out."

"Why? What do we do?"

"Stay back there and put your seat belts on," he said. "I'm gonna try to steer clear of the cars."

The Fiesta picked up speed. My dad honked the horn, but there was nowhere for the cars ahead of us to go. "Hang on," he said, and drove up on to the sidewalk. Tourists leapt out of the way, screaming.

"Sorry!" he yelled as we barreled past. He cut the wheel, taking us into the parking lot of the Golden Gate Bridge Welcome Center. It was filled with tourists, buses, and parked cars. My dad drove the Fiesta through one lane, then down another, laying down the horn constantly and barely missing other cars. We were nearly at the end of the lot when the baby stroller appeared in front of our car. The mother was looking at her phone, and had pushed her child into the lane without checking.

My dad cut the wheel hard to the left. We missed the stroller but were now heading straight for the welcome center. There was no way around it and no way for us to stop. "Brace yourselves!" yelled my dad. I had just enough time to pull on my Superkid helmet and shield my sister. Then our car plowed into the building.

The seat belt cut into my stomach. The already cracked windshield burst inward, spraying us with safety glass. The dashboard bent. My dad's head cracked off the steering wheel. The Fiesta wheezed its last breath, then lay still, nothing more than a smoking, battered hunk of metal now. The old bucket had served us well.

"Washee no nah," said Val. She seemed the most unaffected by our crash. Those infant car seats were no joke.

People were already running over to check on us. I shook my dad's shoulder. "Dad? Are you okay? Dad!"

Blearily, he lifted his head. Blood dribbled from a gash on the bridge of his nose. His right leg was pinned under the crumpled dashboard. When he spoke, his voice was thick and slow. "Robbie. When'd you get so big?"

"Dad, the car is done for. What do we do?"

He tried to blink away his stupor but was only partially successful. "You have to . . . hide. Take your sister, go to the bridge . . . and blend in. Contact . . . contact Fletcher once you're safe."

"I can't," I said. "I can't ditch you and Mom in the same day."

He smiled faintly. "That's . . . the first time . . . you haven't called her Brynn. She'd have . . . liked that."

"Stop being sappy! I can't take these guys on all by myself."

"Sure . . . you can. You two . . . you're Superkids."

I couldn't help but tear up at that. Through the line of concerned tourists, I could see the mercenaries' white van enter the parking lot. They probably wouldn't hurt my dad with so many witnesses, but if my sister was still around, who knew what they would do? I grabbed my Superkid duster and the baby carrier from the back seat, then unbuckled Val from her seat.

"My goodness," said an older woman who was peering in at us. "Are you all right, child?"

"We're fine," I said, strapping Val to my chest. "But my dad needs first aid. Can you call 911?" I cinched on my baby sister's helmet, then pressed a hand to my dad's window. He did the same, gesturing for me to get going.

And even though I hated myself for it, I went. I backed away into the growing crowd, and jogged to the pedestrian walkway that led up to the Golden Gate Bridge. So far, no one had given my Superkid garb a second glance, but I couldn't count on that lasting for too long.

"Mama ma?" asked Val.

I kissed her on the head. "We'll get her back—don't worry, baby girl. But first we need to find a place to hide."

I scanned the bridge's architecture for any kind of nook or crawl space I could cram me and Val into. There weren't many. It was almost like the guys who built the thing didn't want people using it as protection from mercenaries.

I looked upward, my eye following the thick red suspension cables all the way up to the closest tower. The tower platforms would be the ultimate hiding place, if I could figure out some way to reach them. It seemed like the suspension cables led straight there, but the bottoms were blocked off by a ten-foot-high fence with barbed wire at the top. It was enough to prevent the run-of-the-mill bridge daredevil, but not a Superkid.

I stood beneath it, waiting for a moment when all the surrounding people were taking Alcatraz selfies, then I pulled a fun-size bag of Doritos from a duster pocket and ripped them open. Val startled, sending us both straight upward with a high-pitched *boing*. A few people turned at the sound, but we were already high above them.

We touched down on the metal suspension cable, about thirty feet off the bridge surface. So far no one had noticed us. Hopefully, that would continue until I could get us higher up. I took a deep breath, grabbed the guylines to either side of the suspension cable, and began the upward climb.

And that's pretty much where you came in. If you've forgotten all the sweet moves I did, head on back to the first chapter and reread. I'll wait.

All caught up now? Good.

So yeah, after climbing the cable, fighting off two adult mercenaries, and Cirque de Soleil–ing myself and my sister to freedom, we ended up trapped on the tower platform by a gun-toting psycho solider. My dad was right—these guys did not play fair. What else could I do but throw Val at him?

Obviously, it looked bad out of context. But hopefully you know enough about me now to realize I wouldn't just chuck my infant sister at a mercenary without a plan. Which I had.

As she flew toward Creepy Calmy, I shouted the magic words: "BLESS YOU!"

My sister heard me, and she sneezed out an EM blast for the record books. It enveloped the mercenary, flattening the barrel of his Uzi and sending ribbons of electricity skittering all over the metal tower spire.

The soldier flew backward, striking the side of the tower. His skull cracked on the hard surface, then he dropped to the platform and lay in an unconscious pile.

At the same time, the long bungee cord attached to the back of my sister's vest went taut. She recoiled toward me, landing safely back in my arms. Val clapped and cooed like she couldn't wait to do it again.

"Forget it," I told her. "That's an in-case-of-emergencies-only maneuver."

I placed her back in the baby carrier, stepping gingerly around the snoozing soldier and entering the tower access door. As I jogged down the fifteen flights of stairs, I had plenty of time to contemplate my options. Should I go back to the welcome center and see what happened to my dad? Flag down a passing car and have them drive me to the police? Find an Apple store and see if I could contact Fletcher online?

By the time I reached the bridge, I still wasn't sure. Each idea had its own share of risks. The welcome center might still be crawling with Bergerschmidt's thugs. The police would all think Val had been kidnapped. And using the Internet was out, since my secret messages had clearly been intercepted by Bergerschmidt and her Homeland Security thugs.

It turned out none of that mattered, though, because the moment I exited the tower stairwell, the mercenaries' white van skidded to a stop in front of me. Yegor was at the wheel, his face as impassive as ever. I blinked, not sure what I should do, but then Fletcher stuck his wide cheerful face around the bodyguard.

"Well, don't just stand there gawking like some Comic-Con noob," he said. "Get in!"

Still, I didn't move. "But that's their . . . How did you . . . ?"

"Der, we boosted one of their vans. We've been chasing you guys since the Legion of Honor. Now hop in."

"Right." I moved toward them, but Fletcher motioned to the rear.

"No, no, no, the back. That way no one'll see you."

I obeyed, walking around to the rear of the van and opening the windowless door. The interior was padded and reinforced with plastic. There were bench-style seats against each wall, weapons racks that currently stood empty, and on the floor of the van, two bound adults in military vests and black ski masks.

"Don't worry—they won't bother anyone," Fletcher called from the front. "Now get in before they send another squad of psychos after us."

Giving Val a reassuring pat, I stepped into the back of the van.

WHAM! The doors slammed shut behind me. I spun around, but there was no handle on my side. "Fletcher?" I said. "What's going on?"

The only response was the van's engine growling to life. Yegor pulled out into traffic, making me stumble a bit. I walked toward the front cab, banging on the hard plastic wall that separated us. "Fletcher! What are you doing?"

One of the bodies near my feet rolled over. Whoever it was made muffled noises that sounded like "Wooby" or "Lobby." Nervously, I reached down and pulled off the ski mask.

It was my stepmother. Brynn's cheeks were flushed from being under the wool cap and a strip of duct tape was plastered over her mouth, but otherwise she seemed fine. "WOOBY," she said again. "Hum fee."

I pulled off the duct tape. "Ugh, finally," she said. "Now I know why Val spits out her pacifier all the time. Here, let's untie your father."

"Dad?" I rolled over the second body and pulled off the ski mask. His nose was twice its usual size and purple, while the rest of his face was marked with several bruises, but it was him, all right. I pulled the tape off his mouth as well.

"Thanks," he said, struggling to sit up. "I'm sorry I couldn't get you farther away from them."

"It's okay," I told them. "I found Fletcher, and he . . ." I realized what must have happened, and went to pound on the wall separating us from the front seat. "Fletcher, it's Yegor! He's in cahoots with Bergerschmidt. He captured my mom and dad!!"

A panel in the separating wall slid back. Fletcher smiled apologetically. "Hey, buddy. I guess you finally realized what's happening, huh?"

"Yeah," I told him, then lowered my voice. "Your bodyguard is one of the *bad guys*." The big blond Russian continued to drive, seemingly unconcerned by what I was saying.

"Dude, what do you take me for?" asked Fletcher. "You think I'd let a turncoat into my operation? Yegor is, and always has been, working for *me*."

"Then . . . why'd he tie up my parents?" I said. "What's going on?"

My friend sighed. "You're really gonna make me spell it out, aren't you. Okay."

He hit play on his iPhone, and a villainous music sting filled the white van. Fletcher held up one of the mercenary's black ski masks, tapping the flaming bird graphic. "You dig my logo? I commissioned it from this really cool graphic design chick in Portland. I know, the whole 'alter ego' thing is clichéd, but it turns out, there's a good reason the bad guys do that in comic books. You start bending a few laws, and a fake name becomes your best friend."

I'm embarrassed to admit that I still didn't quite follow was going on. In my defense, the kid had been my best friend for three years. My stepmom nudged me.

"Fletcher is the *Phoenix*," she whispered.

Another big music sting filled the van. As Fletcher held up his phone again, the truth hit me like a two-hundred-pound ex-KGB agent. My best friend, the guy who had been with me and Superkid every step of the way—he was the actual villain?

He was the *villain*.

Seeing I'd finally put two and two together, Fletcher spread his hands contritely. "Sorry for all the subterfuge, buddy. But in all fairness to you, I did a really good job hiding everything."

I was still in shock, but Brynn kicked the thick plastic wall that separated us from Fletcher. "You poisoned my baby girl, you maniac!" she shouted. "Your little prank altered her DNA."

"And look at her," said Fletcher. "Able to take down a team of well-trained mercenaries before she can even walk. I call that success."

I struggled to bring my brain back online. "So . . . you irradiated Brynn's prenatal vitamins? How did you know it would give Val superpowers?"

My former best friend shrugged. "To be honest, I didn't. You know I was never much into science. I figured, if it could give an adult short-term powers, maybe it could do even more for a fetus. All I had to do was buy a little chunk of Fortis online, and drop it in your stepmom's vitamin container. But I did not expect her to turn out as awesome as she did."

"Awesome?!" my dad thundered, awkwardly getting to his feet. "You ruined my baby girl's *life*!"

"Mr. Rampino. You should be thanking me." Fletcher actually sounded angry about it. "You know how many people wish their kid was the world's first superhero? I gave you guys a *gift*."

"That's what you call this?" asked my stepmom, cuddling Val to her chest. "You clearly have no idea what we've been dealing with for the last two days."

Fletcher shook his head. "You guys, you're so ungrateful. Robbie discovers his sister has these incredible powers, but does he wanna use them? Noooo. So I had to help him make costumes and create scenarios and invent supervillain personas from scratch, just to drag him this far. And then you two"—he glared at my parents—"you want to get rid of them? Not on my watch."

"Scenarios?" I asked. The blanks were starting to fill in. "So that first guy we rescued in Santa Monica, you pushed him off the pier?"

He spread his hands modestly. "Technically, Yegor pushed him. But *you* were the one who needed the encouragement."

"That means you hired Emilio to take that woman hostage. . . . You suggested we break into Tanzarian's. . . . You were the reason we almost got our faces chewed off by a gampr?!"

Fletcher's expression darkened. "I saw the potential of that meteorite immediately. I was only able to get a small piece of it at first, but once Val proved what it could do, I begged my father to buy the whole thing. Unfortunately, he called my plan a 'frivolous fantasy,' so Tanzarian beat us to it. Which meant we had to steal it back. And it would have worked if Patty hadn't called the police."

"Patty saved your lives, young man," Brynn said. "You were in over your head."

"I had it under control," Fletcher shot back. "Until Bergerschmidt swooped in with her SWAT team and screwed everything up."

More lightbulbs turned on in my brain. "So then . . . she was never the bad guy," I said.

He scoffed. "You think a lame-o like her could pull this off? She did what we needed her to do. She arrested Emilio, pinpointed who bought the meteorite, and scared you guys into going on the run. I just didn't expect her to figure out who the Phoenix was so quickly. That kept us on our toes for a couple of days, huh, Yegor?" The Russian bodyguard's only response was to merge on to the southbound 5.

"You're thirteen," said Brynn. "How—how were you able to do all this by yourself? Where are your parents??"

"Oh, Robbie never told you what my dad's real business is?"

"I thought it was some kind of pharmaceuticals," said my dad.

"Technically, that's true," said Fletcher. "Only, he deals in the illegal kind."

"Your dad is a *drug dealer*?" I'd eaten meals with Rath Grossman. He could be intense, sure, but the guy wore polo shirts. I couldn't picture him as a criminal mastermind.

"Why do you think my parents split up? Or why I never see my mom? How many thirteen-year-olds you know have a personal-driver-slash-bodyguard?"

I had heard enough. "That's it—we're out of here." I lifted my baby sister out of Brynn's arms and pointed her at the back door of the van. "*Bless you*, Val."

WHOOM. The van rattled slightly as my sister sent out an EM blast, but the walls and doors held. I was about to try again, but Fletcher cut me off. "I'd slow your roll there, sidekick. The whole van's lined with reinforced plastic. Like Magneto's prison at the end of *X-Men*. The only way to bust out is to wreck the whole vehicle. And since we're going sixty-five, I bet the only one who survives a crash at that speed is your baby sister."

Angrily, I hand Val back to my stepmom and kicked the plastic partition repeatedly. "You two-faced, self-centered . . . butt-wad!"

He actually looked a little guilty. "I didn't want it to go down like this, buddy. All I wanted was for us to work together, catch bad guys, live the dream. But you didn't want to have any fun."

"Fun?" I asked in disbelief. "Fletcher, people got hurt because of us. They could have died. Putting my sister in harm's way? That's not fun."

He chuckled softly. "You know, all those years reading comics, and I never understood why the bad guy always explains his master plan to the hero. But now that we're here, I get it. It's such a relief to unload." He turned to look at the road ahead. "Now that I know how Fortis works, I'm gonna create a whole league of infant superheroes. A squadron of kids for me to command, just like Professor X. A team against which no gang leader, no warlord, no bully will be able to stand. A gut check for the entire world."

Brynn laughed. "You *are* an only child, aren't you?"

"Yeah, dumbass," I said. "You think you're gonna get a bunch of babies to follow your orders? The point of kids isn't to control 'em. You *can't* control them."

"All you can do is help them grow into quality human beings," agreed my dad. "Which, I'm sorry to say, it looks like your parents failed at. But it's not too late for you, Fletcher."

"That's right, honey," Brynn said. "You don't have to be like your father. You can still do the right thing. Just tell your driver to pull over and let us out."

Fletcher scoffed. "You think this was my dad's idea? Please. He's, like, the least creative person I know. He never saw the potential in Fortis. And man, was he pissed when he found out I dosed Val with it. Thought it would 'disrupt his business' if I got caught. That's all he cares about. But when I showed him what Val could do, he came around. Even agreed to fund my ideas for Phase Two."

"'Phase Two'?" I repeated. "You're nuts if you think we're gonna let you do this to a bunch of other babies."

"Careful now," said Fletcher. "You don't wanna rush to judgment on something that'll affect the rest of your life. I suggest you sleep on it." He pushed a green button on the van's dashboard. Nothing happened. He pressed it again, saying, "*Sleep* on it."

Still, nothing happened. He turned to Yegor. "Did you disconnect the gas line?" The Russian grunted and shook his head.

Fletcher thumped the dashboard, pressing the button several times in quick succession. "Oooh, scary," I said sarcastically. "You want us to sleep, maybe try a lullaby instead."

Fletcher stuck his thick arm under the seat, fiddling with some kind of canister. "Aha!" he said triumphantly. "The release valve wasn't opened. So as I was saying . . . *sleep on it.*" He hit the green button again.

There was a hissing sound as invisible gas began to filter into the rear compartment of the white van. Fletcher gave us a wave, then shut the small access panel. My parents and I covered our mouths, but the hissing continued. It smelled sweet and cold, like the sleeping gas I'd had once at the dentist's office. Val sneezed, making the vehicle rattle briefly. The walls of the van blurred slightly, then solidified.

I turned to my parents. My dad and Brynn were swaying on their feet. "It's no-trous ixeed," slurred my father. "Natrox newside." He sat heavily on one of the benches, giggling. "Nitrous. Oxide. We can't . . . stop . . ." Still laughing, he slumped over and closed his eyes.

Brynn took me by the shoulders. "We'll get out of this," she said, suppressing her own laughter. "We just have to . . . stick . . . stick . . ." But then she also dropped.

It was just me and Val left. I looked blearily down at my sister to see she'd fallen asleep too. For some reason, it seemed hilarious. Everything did, even the thought of taking on Fletcher all by myself. I'd just unscrew one of the back doors, use it to surf down the freeway, lasso one of them thar emergency call boxes, and contact Homeland . . . Homeland . . .

I blinked, realizing I'd somehow ended up on my back at the rear of the van. My baby sister was snoozing on my chest. Not a bad idea. I'd close my eyes just for a second, grab some quick bit of shut-eye, then I'd be refreshed and ready to fight my best friend. My friend, the bad guy. My good humor evaporated.

"Fletcher . . ." I murmured sadly.

Then my eyes closed, and the van went dark.

I woke to the screech of metal grinding on metal. The rear doors of the white van were being pried open. Evidently, Val's EM blast had had at least some small effect on the plastic-lined vehicle.

I sat up. My baby sister was still asleep, and strapped to my chest in the same position as the day before. My back throbbed from where the baby carrier straps had pressed into my muscles. My head pounded with every scrape of metal. Best of all, there was a large wet patch on my stomach. Apparently Val's diaper had leaked while she was asleep, and now we were both drenched in pee.

There was one final metallic death-scream. Bright early morning sunlight filled the back of the van as the doors swung wide. I used a hand to shield my eyes. Five silhouettes stood outside. Four were muscled ski-mask-wearing, Uzi-carrying mercenaries. The other was Fletcher.

"Up and at 'em," he said brightly.

My dad and Brynn stirred, also groaning in pain. "How long did you leave the nitrous on for?" said my dad, cradling his head.

Fletcher shrugged. "I don't know, a couple hours? Like I said, I'm not a scientist."

Val also woke, immediately crying in discomfort. If we all had headaches, I couldn't imagine how she felt. I found a spare pacifier in my utility belt and popped it in her mouth. She continued to fuss, but at least now it was mildly muffled.

"Now, the three of you have a decision to make," said Fletcher. "You can get out of the van and quietly come with me, or these guys are gonna shoot you. And I know only one of you can deflect bullets."

I looked at my parents. I could tell by their faces that now was not the time to fight. I lifted my hands and obediently scooted out of the van.

We were in a boring, nondescript parking lot. A large three-story white warehouse stood directly in front of us. On the far side of the complex was an indoor playground, with a furniture storage facility beside it. Both were closed at the moment.

"What, no secret volcano base?" I asked. I thought being snarky might keep my increasing fear at bay. "Laaaaame."

"I know, it's not much to look at," admitted Fletcher. "But my dad likes to keep a low profile."

When we reached the front entrance, he placed his hand on a biometric scanner, then typed in a four-digit code. The door unlocked, and he gestured for us to go inside. We went past a reception area with a sign that read PHOENIX PHARMACEUTICALS, continued through a clutch of boring, corporate-style offices, then came to a halt at a door labeled FACTORY FLOOR—RESTRICTED ACCESS! Fletcher entered another code to unlock the door, then held it open for us.

Inside was a large open-plan production facility. There were more offices against the back wall, and a central glass-walled observation room suspended above the factory floor. A complex web of conveyor belts, manned by workers in white biohazard suits, filled the space. At the center of the web, in a shielded glass case, was Fortis. The meteorite shone with that strange, shimmery blue-green light. As rows of plastic bottles passed beneath it, a sliver of the meteorite was chipped off, then the bottles were filled with yellow pills. These were sealed by the workers and then stacked in boxes labeled PRENATAL VITAMINS—FOR IMMEDIATE SHIPMENT.

"All of those pills . . . they're being irradiated with Fortis?" Brynn sounded ill at the thought of it.

"They are," replied a warm, confident voice. Rath Grossman came toward us, a broad smile stretched across his face. His powerful frame was encased in tan slacks and a blue golf shirt. His bald crown gleamed in the factory light.

"Rath Grossman," he said to my parents, pronouncing his first name as "Wraith" and extending his hand. "Fletcher's told me all about you and your family."

Neither my dad nor Brynn took his hand. Fletcher's dad withdrew it, but continued his easygoing smile. "I understand your trepidation, considering what you've all been through these last few days. I know we've had a rocky beginning, but my son assures me we all have similar desires."

"Your son is wrong," said Brynn. "Especially if it involves poisoning a bunch of pregnant women without their knowledge."

"Yeah," I added. "After everything he's done, we're basically enemies."

Fletcher's gaze dropped to the floor. Rath turned to glower at his son. "Yes, he informed me how this situation began. You should know, I don't believe in lying to my friends. You have my deepest apologies that he didn't come clean sooner." He squeezed his son's shoulder, making Fletcher wince. "However. Ill-advised as his little 'experiment' was, it turned out to be an incredible success. One that, I believe, has already redefined the world. A world with superpowers."

He took Val's tiny hands in his. I pulled her back, but he merely smiled again. "Obviously, we can't expect this little girl to shoulder such a burden all by herself. We need to cast a wider net." He turned to indicate the busy factory. "Thankfully, my business had the resources to make use of Armin Tanzarian's little purchase."

My dad cleared his throat. "So . . . your plan is to re-create what your son did to my baby, without the parents' knowledge, only on a larger scale?"

"Precisely. If we told people the pills were irradiated, we wouldn't get very many takers. But our deeply discounted, prenatal 'vitamins' already have several customers lined up through the indoor playground next door. In another year or so, we hope to have a dozen Superkids."

"And when the babies start shooting laser beams from their eyes or transforming into rubber, who will their parents turn to for help?" Fletcher asked quickly. "The world's only experts on the subject." He jabbed both of his thumbs toward himself.

"Wow," I said as sarcastically as possible. "You guys really are villains. Congratulations."

Rath surveyed us, pressing his fingertips together. "I think they need a little time to digest. And we have just the place."

He beckoned us toward the back wall of the factory. My parents and I resisted, until the mercenaries poked us with their Uzis.

We grudgingly followed Rath and Fletcher across the factory. Several of the workers looked up, but evidently they were used to the presence of armed guards and hostages, because each one of them went back to their work. We came to a row of offices connected by a long, single hallway. Rath led us through an employee break room stocked with vending machines, past a few locked storage areas, and came to a stop outside a thick, see-through plastic door. One of the guards opened it and ushered us inside. There was a table, a few chairs, two air mattresses, and a plastic shelf filled with baby products.

"Home sweet ho-ome," Fletcher sang off-key.

"What my son means to say," said Rath, giving him another look of annoyance, "is that we had this room built especially for your daughter. The walls, floor, and ceiling are composed of six-inch reinforced plastic. As is the furniture. There's not a scrap of metal within thirty yards of this room."

"So what do you expect us to do?" asked Brynn. "Just sit in here until we change our minds about helping you? 'Cause that is not gonna happen."

My dad and I nodded our agreement. "I know we got off on the wrong foot," said Rath, "but I think it's best for everybody if we work together. For starters, me and the boys don't change diapers." The mercenaries chuckled. "Secondly, your alternatives are not great."

He gestured to one of his men. Because of the ski mask, I couldn't be sure which one it was. But he moved like Creepy Calmy. He leveled his Uzi at my stepmother.

"Hold on," said my dad. He stepped forward, shielding Brynn with his hands. "You don't have to do this. We can—"

CRACK. There was a short, sharp sound as Creepy Calmy pulled the trigger of his Uzi. A single bullet ripped through the palm of my dad's left hand, leaving behind a spray of red and imbedding itself in the far plastic wall. My dad looked down at the hole in shock. Brynn grabbed a clean diaper from a nearby shelf as Val began to wail.

"What is wrong with you?!" my stepmom asked, pressing the absorbent cloth against his wound. "We haven't done anything!"

Seeing her distress, Val intensified her cries. Rath stepped forward, his expression cold. "Consider it an incentive. I want all three of you to carefully consider our proposal. Work with us, and you can continue to raise your daughter. Refuse, and . . ." He shrugged.

"Why are you doing this?" I asked Fletcher. He looked at little green at the sight of my dad's maimed hand. "We were *friends*."

He swallowed uneasily, glancing at his father. Rath's face was impassive. "Yeah, well, some things are more important," Fletcher said. "You'll figure that out someday."

He, his father, and their goons left. One of the mercenaries locked the heavy plastic door behind them. Brynn guided my dad to a plastic chair, while I finally pulled Val out of the baby carrier. Her wails went away once she took in her new environment. As my sister began crawl around our prison cell, I inspected the few items at our disposal. The chairs were flimsy and light, and the small amount of silverware was all cheap plastic. There was nothing that could help us escape, but at least I could give Val a fresh diaper. As I changed her, my stepmom gently probed my dad's bloody hand.

"How is it?" she asked him.

"Not too bad," he said. "But I don't think I'll be punching my way out of here."

"So what do we do?" I asked, cinching the new diaper around Val and buttoning up her onesie. I set her down to crawl again. "Fletcher and his nutjob father have thought of everything."

"We can't let them take Val," said my father. "Those two will use her like a child soldier." We all looked at my baby sister, who had pulled herself to a standing position by a box of squeezy pouches. One by one, she began pulling them out.

"So what, then?" Brynn asked. "They clearly have no problem shooting us."

None of us said anything for a while. Val crawled over to the center of the room, softly babbling to herself. I was fairly confident that we were doomed. Warm salt water filled my eyes, but I blinked it away. I had never cried in front of Brynn, and I wasn't about to start now.

"This is all my fault," I said. "All that stuff about wanting to do good, help the world—that was crap. I wanted be a superhero, so I let

Fletcher talk me into everything. I should have never used Val's powers. At least not until she could decide for herself how to use 'em. I'm—I'm sorry." I really was. Rath's mercenaries would come back eventually, shoot us dead, then give my innocent baby sister to a psychotic teenager who had been my best friend. I wiped tear stains off my cheeks. So much for looking tough in front of my stepmom.

Brynn and my dad wrapped their arms around me. "You couldn't have known what he was really planning," she said soothingly. "I've seen it in court all the time. No matter how well we think we know someone, people are capable of anything. Especially when their priorities are screwed up."

"Or when they're forced into it," said my dad. "Fletcher might have irradiated our prenatal vitamins, but I think Rath is the one responsible for all this."

"Yeah, I really don't trust that guy," I said. "But how are we gonna get out of here?"

A low metallic *bong* sounded through the room. We all turned to see Val had flown twenty feet into the air, and was currently stuck to a metal air vent in the ceiling.

"Whoa!" said Brynn, running over to stand underneath her daughter. She held out her arms to catch her. "It's okay, honey. Just demagnetize and Mama will catch you."

"Hold on a second," I said. "If that vent is metal, she might be able to open it."

"It's ten inches wide," said my dad. "Even if we could get up there, we can't fit through that."

"But she can," I pointed out.

"She's a *baby*," Brynn replied. "She can't make decisions or take care of herself. She can't do anything!"

"Yes, she can," I insisted, and looked up to my sister. "Bless you, Val. Bless you! Bless—"

"Bleh boo!" my sister repeated. There was a familiar *thrum* as her EM field blasted outward. The vent cover popped off. Val shot up into the small hole and disappeared into darkness.

"Val?" my stepmom called up at the air vent. Her voice was tight with worry. "Honey, are you okay?"

"Bunga bunga ba ba," came the eleven-month-old's voice. There were some metal bangs and bongs, then more nonsense exclamations.

"Come on down," said my dad, trying to sound calm. "Come on, little girl."

There was a grunt, more muffled bangs, and then a cry of frustration.

"Oh my God, she's stuck," said Brynn. She was literally pacing in circles now. "She's stuck—what do we do?" She called up to the vent. "Valeria Cooper Rampino, you come down this instant!"

My baby sister laughed. There were more metal thumps, a bass-y *thrum*, then the air vent cover in the hallway ceiling clattered to the floor. As we all ran to the see-through plastic door, Val dropped out of opening and bounced a few times on the floor. Seeing the three of us gape at her, she gave a big gummy smile. She swung her right arm around in her best imitation of a wave.

"Hi, baby," I said. "See, I knew she could do it. Good job, Val!"

Brynn rounded on me. "She's out there and we're in here. How is that a 'good job'?"

"Just hold on," I told her. "Can you open the door for us, Valley? Come open the door."

"Oogie ba," said my sister. Placing her chubby hands on the floor, she slowly but steadily pushed herself to her feet. There she stood, swaying slightly, but standing for the first time all on her own.

"Holy crap, she can stand?" said my dad. "Since when can she stand?"

"Good job, baby girl!" I applauded. Val smiled at me, clapping her little hands in response. "Now walk over here and open this door."

Shakily, but with great purpose, my baby sister put her right foot forward. Her forehead wrinkled in concentration. Then her left foot went forward. Right foot . . . left foot . . . she tilted, but stayed upright. Unfortunately, she was heading away from us, toward the featureless wall across the way.

"Good Lord, she can walk now too?" said Brynn. She put a hand to her mouth. "My baby girl can walk."

"And of course we have no cameras," complained my dad. "Good job, honey! Take those steps!"

"Actually, can you turn around, Valley?" I called. "Come on, sweetie, come back this way."

My sister stopped, bracing herself against the wall. Pooching out her lower lip, she took a series of mini shuffle-steps until she was again facing us. All three of us now burst into applause.

"Okay, she's officially a genius," said my dad proudly.

Brynn teared up. "Our baby girl's all grown up."

"I think you have a little time until she leaves for college," I said dryly. "Now walk toward us, Valley. Come on. Walk over and grab the doorknob." I jiggled it to get her attention.

"Do na," Val echoed, then began toddle back toward us. She was more confident now, grinning and moving with her arms held out like a mini gymnast. One, two, three, four steps—and my sister fell flat on her face.

We gasped. There was a long, tension-filled silence—

Then Val screamed. She lifted her face to look at us, her cute, squishy features red and contorted with fear, pain, or both.

"It's okay," my dad said. "Everybody falls, baby."

"Yeah, you're not bleeding or anything," I added. "Just get back up and grab that doorknob. Door, Valley. DOOR."

Val took a shuddering breath, but her cries reduced to a mild fussing. Cautiously, she pushed herself up onto her knees. "That's it," said Brynn encouragingly. "You got this, honey."

With a grunt, my baby sister pushed herself back into a standing position. We whooped and cheered. Val took a few steps forward, placing her hand on the plastic door lever.

"Now pull it down," I said, miming the action for her. "Pull, pull, pull."

"Puh," repeated Val. She mimicked my movements, but the handle didn't budge.

"It's a plastic lock," said my dad. "I was worried about this. We can't open it without a key."

"The guards. They all had keys," I said. "I saw them on those retractable belt thingies."

"So now we want a toddler to take down an adult mercenary?" asked Brynn.

"She's done it before," I replied.

"But not by herself!"

"She's already out there. What else can we do?"

"Bring her back inside," said Brynn. "When the guards show up, we can have her zap their guns or something."

"I think Robbie's right," said my dad. "This might be our only shot at getting out. Worst case scenario, they catch her and put her back in here."

"No, the worst case scenario is we all get shot," said Brynn. "But I suppose it's safer than trying to deflect bullets." My stepmom squatted down, placing her hands on the see-through door and making eye contact with her daughter. "Okay, hon. We need you to find a guard? And take his key." She mimed holding one. "KEY."

Val giggled, smacking the door with her palms. I crouched next to Brynn. "Key, Valley. Go that way and find a key." I gestured to my dad, who handed me his key ring. I jingled them for Val to see. "KEY. Find one just like this."

"Ka ka ka!" said Val.

"That way," I said, pointing down the hallway.

My kid sister gurgled, but started toddling in the right direction. "Good girl!" called Brynn. "You can do it, sweetie."

Plop. Val fell to the floor again. She looked back at us in concern. "That's okay," I said, putting on a big smile for her benefit. "No big deal, just get back up. Uppy-uppy."

The baby pushed herself back to her feet. She took another step forward—

Then fell again.

"Why doesn't she just crawl?" said my dad. "She'll never get there this way."

"It's a brand-new skill," Brynn admonished him. "She needs to learn through reinforcement."

"Like we need any more suspense here," I said, then called down the hall. "Come on, kiddo. Work those footsies!"

Champion that she was, Val got to her feet for the third time that morning. Brynn whooped. "Yes! Walk that walk, baby girl."

Step by step, Val toddled down the hallway until she reached the break room. By mushing my face against the far edge of our see-through prison door, I could just barely see what was going on. A young, simple-looking guard stood in the lounge, staring at a soda machine.

"Ka," Val said, making Simple Guard turn. He dropped his change on seeing my sister.

"Whoa," he said. "How'd you get out?"

Val gurgled, putting a fist in her smiling mouth. "What is she doing?" said my dad, also pressing his face against our prison door. "Attack him, attack."

But my kid sister merely smiled at the mercenary from around her fist. "She's too nice. She gets that from your side," I said to Brynn. "Zero killer instinct."

"She can take him," said my stepmom, trying to get a better angle of the break room. "Bless you, Val. BLESS YOU."

But the baby couldn't hear us. She actually cooed as Simple Guard picked her up. "Best put you back before I get in trouble," he said, and began walking toward us.

"Unbelievable," I said. Then I called through the door, "You're making us all look bad!"

Simple Guard reached the other side of our prison, seeing us all standing there. "Okay, guys. Lift your hands and back up so I can open the door."

We did so, keeping our hands where he could see them. He shifted Val to the crook of his left arm, inserting a plastic key into the door lock.

"Bless you, Val," said my dad. "Bless you."

"No funny business, now," the simpleton said. "I had a whole briefing on how y'all activate her powers. You want me to hurt her?"

"BLESS YOU, VAL," said Brynn.

"I'm serious," the guard said. "I'll hurt her."

"BLESS YOU, BLESS YOU, BLESS YOU!" I yelled.

The guard winced, but nothing happened. He scowled. "Okay, now. No more talking, or I'll take her straight to—"

THRUM. Val magnetized her body, sending her and Simple Guard straight up. He smacked into the ceiling, but thankfully hung on to my sister. They both dropped back to the floor. Val chuckled, but he shook his head, a little woozy.

"Now listen," he said. "I told you not to—"

WHOOM. Now Val sent out an EM blast. Simple Guard flew backward, his thin skull cracking against the opposite wall. My sister slipped to the hallway floor, landing safely on her butt. The poor guard looked at us in confusion, then staggered forward and slumped against the door, unconscious.

I ran forward to try the handle, but it was still locked. His key was still in the door, but he hadn't turned it. "No!" I shouted, pounding on the thick plastic with my fists. "We're so close!"

Simple Guard's slack face slid down the see-through plastic, squeaking as it slowly descended. His left elbow came to rest on top of the key. All three of us held our breath as his weight excruciatingly, painstakingly began to press down on the key.

Click. It turned. The plastic lock sprang open, and the guard's weight swung the door inward.

As one, we ran forward. My dad pulled the guard inside, while Brynn scooped up Val and showered her with kisses. "You were so, so, so brave," she said to the gurgling baby. "I am so proud of you!"

"I told you, she's a natural," I said.

My dad quickly searched the guard, setting aside his MAC-10 Uzi, a ring of keys, a wallet, and the dude's iPhone.

"Is there a signal?" Brynn said upon seeing the phone. "We should call 911."

"Good idea," said my dad, "however." He turned the screen toward us. It was smashed and impossible to read.

I took it from him, trying to get the screen to respond. No dice. "It must've gotten crushed when Val launched him into the wall," I lamented.

"A phone's not gonna save us," my dad said. "What we need is to get out of here."

"And how do we do that?" asked Brynn, kissing Val's fuzzy head. "There's a whole factory of guns and guards between us and the exit."

"We could split up," I suggested. "Dad and I will create a diversion or something, while you get Val to safety."

"And have Fletcher's dad shoot you both? No way," said my stepmom. "Just 'cause people split up in the movies, doesn't mean it works. We're a family—we stick together."

My dad smiled at me. "Super Family. It does have a ring to it."

I held out my hand for a fist bump. My dad and then Brynn joined in. "Let's just all avoid getting killed, okay?" she asked.

I helped her put on the baby carrier and load up Val, while my dad hefted the MAC-10. "You know how to use one of those things?" I asked him.

In answer, he pulled back the slide and chambered a bullet with the confidence of Jason Bourne. "I was playing first-person shooters before you were born," he replied.

As one, we stepped out of our plastic prison.

The first few minutes of our escape were anticlimactic. There were no security cameras to avoid, no laser defense systems to dodge, not even a lone henchmen with some kind of weird physical trait to tangle with. We simply crept down a boring office hallway, in which all the doors were closed and all the handles were locked.

Things picked up when we reached the employee break room. An unsuspecting factory employee in a yellow biohazard suit was pouring creamer into a cup of coffee, her back to us. Sensing my family's presence, she turned. We all stared at one another, frozen.

Then the factory worker dropped her coffee and ran for the door. Brynn bent down and blew gently on Val's face. My baby sister scrunched up her little nose and sneezed. An EM blast spread through the tiny room, knocking aside chairs and tables. The poor employee was knocked off her feet, smacking headfirst into the doorframe. She slid to the floor, unconscious.

"Well, that wasn't so tough," I said. "A couple more henchpeople like that, and we'll be home free."

My dad dragged the employee under a table. "I wouldn't get too cocky. Some of the other henchpeople here have guns."

Brynn passed Val to him. We left the break room and stepped out onto the second-floor catwalk that overlooked the factory floor. The production line was in full swing, with bright yellow pills being funneled into bottles and a few dozen workers boxing the Fortis-irradiated results. Eight of the Grossmans' ski-masked, gun-toting mercenaries patrolled the warehouse at various points. And unfortunately, one of those points was about five feet ahead of us.

The mercenary saw us and lifted his Uzi. Quickly, I reached down to tickle Val's feet. She giggled and squirmed. *Thrum.* The metal catwalk buzzed, and the mercenary's gun was yanked from his hand by my sister's EM field. It hung, suspended in the air, halfway between us. The mercenary stretched out a hand toward his Uzi—

And I tickled Val again. She squealed, and the Uzi flew back toward its owner. It clocked him in the face. He staggered backward, his butt striking the catwalk railing. His arms flailed. He tipped over—

And fell off the catwalk. Thankfully, there was a pallet of cardboard pill boxes directly beneath him. These he hit. The boxes tumbled across the factory floor, breaking open and scattering pill bottles everywhere. All the nearby factory workers turned toward the sound. One enterprising individual even decided to shut down the factory line. The conveyor belts shuddered to a stop, and the warehouse became deathly quiet. Three dozen workers stared up at us.

So much for making a stealthy exit. It was time to improvise.

I took a step forward and cleared my throat. "Hi there. Just so everyone knows, we've called the police." I held up Simple Guard's phone. "They're on their way here, but they only care about your boss. Anyone who doesn't wanna be arrested should leave now."

There was a beat as the workers looked at one another. Collectively, they decided that prison time wasn't worth their hourly wage. They all began to jog for the exits.

"Nicely done," my dad whispered. He clapped me on the shoulder. Brynn kissed me on the cheek. "Yeah, next time I need to make opening statements on a case, you're hired."

Unfortunately, the eight mercenaries must have been better paid. They moved toward us, Uzis in hand. Two of them fired.

I wrapped my arms around my parents. "Group hug!" I shouted, and jumped off the catwalk. Bullets pinged off the metal walls where our heads had been. We dropped toward the concrete floor.

"What are you doing?" asked my dad.

"Boo!" I said right into Val's face.

She gasped. Six inches from breaking our anklebones, there was a high-pitched *boing*. We repelled off the ground, flew through the factory, and stuck to the side of a metal vat. I tickled my sister under her arms, making her demagnetize. We dropped back down to the floor—

And found ourselves right in front of another mercenary. My dad was the first to react, blowing gently on Val's face. Her nose twitched, she sneezed, and *WHOOM*—an EM blast knocked the dude back ten feet.

Brynn tapped me on the shoulder. "Behind you."

We turned to see another mercenary running toward us, gun in hand. He was ten feet away, but any bullets he fired would reach us much faster.

"Tickle, tickle, tickle," said my stepmom in a high-pitched voice, stroking the soft soles of her daughter's feet.

Val chortled. *Thrum*—the approaching guard's Uzi was yanked forward. To his credit, he refused to let go. His weapon dragged him across the concrete floor. There was a heavy *thwack* as his head smacked against a metal column. Then he, too, went down for the count.

"Over there," said my dad, pointing to another approaching mercenary.

I lifted Val out of my dad's arms, placed her on the slick factory floor, and pushed. She slid toward the surprised guard, coming to a stop right in front of him.

"Bless you!" I called. The resulting EM blast sent him straight up. His skull pinged off the underbelly of a conveyor belt like a Ping-Pong ball, and he fell back to the ground in a crumpled heap.

While I ran to collect my sister, Brynn pulled out the nozzle from a diesel pump near one of the main belts. I have no idea why such a thing was there—maybe the conveyor belts were gas-powered?—but it came in handy for us. My stepmom sprayed fuel on to the conveyor belt of pills. It spilled down the length of the factory's rubber belt network. Then she aimed the Uzi we'd taken from Simple Guard at the yellow pills, and pulled the trigger.

The conveyor belt erupted in flames. Fire quickly spread through the warehouse, separating us from a few of the remaining mercenaries.

But not all of them. As I scooped up Val, another ski-masked psycho stepped from behind a column. He was bulkier than his buddies, and his Uzi was at the ready. His eyeballs vibrated like two black marbles with ADHD.

"Are you really gonna shoot us?" I said. "I don't think your boss would be too happy if his only Superkid got hurt."

Bulky Bob smiled. "That's true. But he also said *you* were expendable."

He fired.

A bloom of fire burst forth from his Uzi's barrel, making both me and my sister wince. Through the roar of gunfire, I heard a bass-y *fwom.*

In the silence that followed, I realized I was uninjured. I cracked an eye to see five bullets hovering in midair about ten inches from my face. I looked down at my baby sister in amazement.

"Uh-uh," she said with the cutest of scowls. She swept her hand sideways, and the bullets went flying. So, too, did Bulky Bob's Uzi. He considered that development, then decided to head for the hills. Two more mercenaries followed his lead.

I laughed. "Did you see that?" I called to my parents. "Val can stop bullets!"

My dad jogged over, lifting my sister out of my hands. "Wonderful. Let's not make a habit out of that."

He slid my sister back toward Brynn, who used another Val-directed EM blast to take out one more mercenary. By my count, that was seven bad guys down. I couldn't see any sign of the eighth. "Looks like we won," I said, then wished I hadn't.

Alarms blared and emergency lights flashed as smoke from Brynn's conveyor belt fire reached the sprinkler system. Water began spraying from overhead nozzles, quickly soaking our clothes. One of the conveyor belts collapsed. It made a huge crash, but worse, my dad and I were now separated from Brynn and Val. I peered upward through the indoor rain to see two silhouettes moving in the overhead office. Looked like Fletcher and his dad were finally aware of what was going on down here.

"Time to go. The exit's right over there." My dad gestured for Brynn and Val to meet us at the open loading dock. A gray delivery truck and two factory golf carts were parked nearby.

"What about Fletcher and his dad?" I said, looking back up at the office. "We're just gonna let them get away?"

"Yes," my dad replied, ushering me toward the loading dock. "You and your sister have done enough for one summer. Real law enforcement can take it from here."

I let myself be pulled toward the open door. We only got about five feet when a figure dropped to the ground in front of us. The guy stood, revealing a muscle-cut six-foot-three mercenary in a Phoenix ski mask. There was something familiar about him, and it wasn't just the Uzi in his hand.

He pulled off his black mask, revealing a scarred, crew-cutted face, with blue eyes that glittered like chips of ice. Yegor.

"Finally," he said in his heavily accented voice. "I no longer must listen to your boring, constant superhero talk. I could shoot you both and be done . . . but where is fun in that?"

He tossed aside his weapon and removed a tiny glass vial from his pocket. The inside was half-filled with glowing blue-green dust the exact hue of Fortis. He unscrewed the cap, tapping a line of the meteorite dust on the back of his left hand.

"Hey, you don't need to do that," said my dad, trying to keep the nervousness from his voice. "You can just let us go and be on your way. We won't tell the authorities what we know about you."

"Yeah, winners don't use drugs, remember?" I added.

Yegor ignored us both, snorting the line of ground-up rock. He reacted as if he'd inhaled chili powder. His pupils grew large and began to vibrate like beans on a hot plate. He exhaled, then crushed the empty glass vial to powder in his fist.

My dad stepped in front of me. "Robbie, run. I'll stall him." I took a couple steps back, but lingered to see if my dad needed help. "You really want to go down with the Grossmans?" my dad asked the approaching driver. "You just work for them. You don't have to believe in their crazy plan—"

CRACK. Yegor's fist shot forward in a blink-and-you-miss-it blur, coldcocking my dad's jaw. His head snapped back, and my father dropped to the floor, unconscious. Not good.

"Stupid man. I work for Grossmans *because* of crazy plan." The driver/mercenary rolled his neck, popping what sounded like a dozen vertebrae. His vibrating blue eyes landed on me. "And now you are all mine, *sidekick*."

I ran. Back into the maze of burning conveyors, dodging dangling rubber belts, metal columns, and a Biblical flood of water from the sprinkler system. Yegor walked after me with the incessant speed and menace of a Terminator. I hid behind a column and looked across the warehouse, hoping Brynn had made it to the loading dock. But she and Val were dealing with their own problems. In an effort to go around the flaming wreckage, my stepmom had tucked Val under one arm and her Uzi under the other, then climbed a ladder back up to the second story catwalk. There she'd encountered Rath Grossman, who held a Glock 9-mm pistol in his hand. Fletcher fidgeted nervously behind him. Brynn and my sister were trapped.

Rath gestured to the burning warehouse with his handgun. "It appears you've chosen your side. I have to say, I'm disappointed."

"Better get used to that feeling," said Brynn. "Especially in prison."

"You know, smart-ass remarks like that used to bother me? Then I discovered guns." Fletcher's dad pointed the Glock. "One tug of the trigger, and you can make anybody shut their mouth."

BAM! He shot my stepmom in the calf. She fell to her knees, dropping the Uzi to the floor below but hanging on to my sister.

"What are you doing?!" said Fletcher, stepping in front of his dad. "You promised me that we wouldn't hurt them anymore!"

Rath shoved his son aside. "Grow up, you pansy. They're our enemies. If your enemy tries to fight you, you don't talk to them and negotiate. You fight back until every single one of them is gone." He placed a foot on Brynn's leg, pulling Val from my stepmom's hands.

Val cried out, reaching for her mom. Brynn struggled to get to her feet, but the pain was too great. Rath shoved the baby into Fletcher's arms. "Looks like you're on diaper duty after all. Now shut her up."

While Fletcher tried to soothe my fussy sister, Rath turned back to my stepmom. "You all, you could have ruled the world. Instead you chose a family. What a waste." He snapped his fingers at his son, then strode away down the catwalk. Fletcher gave Brynn an apologetic, torn look, then trotted after his father.

My stepmom pulled herself up to a sitting position, and spotted me peering out from my hiding place. Her face was streaked with pain. "Robbie! They're taking Val!!"

Her words rang across the warehouse, but at the moment I couldn't do much about them. Flames surrounded my hiding place on the three sides, and the space above me was blocked by the underside of a massive metal vat filled with loose pills. The smoke from the still-burning gasoline fire made it difficult to breathe. And I knew Yegor was only a few yards away, between me and my only escape route.

I glanced back toward the loading dock, seeing Fletcher and his dad load Val into the gray delivery truck. The back was filled with boxed-up ready-to-sell prenatal "vitamins" that would create potentially hundreds more superpowered babies. Rath shut the rear doors, then went around to start the vehicle.

My eyes watered from the increasing smoke around me. My lungs burned. I knew if I coughed, it would be all over. I scanned the nearby area for anything that might help. Some rubber hoses, a tiny fire extinguisher, a release lever for the vat above me . . . nothing I could use as a real weapon.

I coughed.

I couldn't help it. You try holding your breath in a factory full of burning rubber, and see how long you last.

Yegor turned slowly toward me. His terrifying smile shone white through the red smoke and sprinkler system water. "Do not feel bad," he said. "Some people, they are meant for warrior lifestyle. And some are not."

"Good," I said. "'Cause I don't want to be anything like you maniacs."

The driver's icy smile twisted into a scowl. He ran at me, lightning-quick, his thick fingers straining to grab me by the neck and squeeze—

But I pulled down the vat release lever. A metal flap above us opened, and river of yellow pills burst forth. The force of it knocked Yegor to the ground. They battered his neck and shoulders like a millions tiny pebbles. He attempted to stand, but his feet were unable to find purchase in the growing mound of yellow beneath him. One arm stretched out toward me, but the yellow downpour beat him to the ground. The pills quickly covered the driver's legs, then his torso, and finally his rage-filled, jittery blue eyes. Only his right hand was left free. As the last pill fell, even that went still.

"Told you," I said to his motionless fingertip. "Winners don't do drugs."

I ran back through burning conveyor belts to my dad. He had revived enough to let me help him stand. "Where's Brynn? And Val?"

"Don't worry—they haven't gotten away with her yet," I told him.

Together, we ran toward the loading dock. Brynn met up with us halfway. She had managed to cinch her belt around her leg as a tourniquet and lower herself down the ladder. But walking was still a problem, so she threw an arm over my shoulder.

With the three of us supporting one another, we made it to the loading dock. Val had been buckled into the front seat of the delivery van and Rath had just started the engine. Fletcher stood beside the vehicle, staring at us.

"What are you waiting for?" Rath bawled at his son. "They don't have any guns—get in!"

"You're really gonna do this?" I called to my former friend. "Kidnap my baby sister? Poison a bunch of pregnant moms? You're not a supervillain, Fletch."

Fletcher looked to his glaring father, then back at me. "What am I supposed to do? He's my dad."

"And he doesn't give a crap about you!" I said. "He never even spent more than five minutes with you until he found out you had access to a superpowered baby."

"Fletcher," Rath said in a calm but threatening voice. "Get in the van. Now."

Brynn took a step forward. "You don't have to help him, hon. Family is what you make it."

"But you'll only ever have one father," said Rafe. "And he is getting pissed. So get in. The van."

Fletcher looked at me, then his father. "No," he said softly.

The top of Rafe's bald head turned purple. "What did you say to me?"

"No," Fletcher said louder. "I'm not kidnapping my best friend's sister so you can rule the world. Robbie's right. They've been more of a real family to me than you ever were."

As far as I knew, it was the first time Fletcher had ever stood up to his father. Rath struggled with that for a moment, and then he shrugged. "Fine. You were never the son I wanted, anyway."

As Fletcher absorbed that awful remark, Rath put the delivery van into drive. He stomped on the gas, speeding out of the burning factory and taking my baby sister with him.

I grabbed my former best friend by the shoulders. "What was that? You call that stopping him?!"

My former friend stared at the empty loading dock, stricken. "He left. He actually left me."

"Yeah, and he took *my* sister. Where'd they go? Think!"

Fletcher shook his head, his eyes filling with tears. "Does it look like he tells me anything?"

Even though it must have hurt like crazy, Brynn bent down on her injured leg and looked him in the eye. "You must have heard something. Seen something. What were his plans after this? Where was he going?"

"I don't know. . . . I saw an email about a private airline company. Just outside San Jose. Escape . . . something with escape in the name. But I don't know where he was going. Or even if he was planning to take me. Probably not." He wiped his eyes with the heel of his hand.

I turned to my dad. "What do we do? How do you think we get Val back?"

He hopped into one of the golf carts and turned it on. "She's family. We go after her."

Less than a minute later, the golf cart squealed out of the Fortis factory. My dad was behind the wheel, I rode shotgun, and Brynn was in the back seat with her injured leg up. She had insisted on coming. Fletcher was still in shock, so we left him at the loading dock. Besides, even though he'd kind of stood up for us, I still didn't trust him. I doubted that I ever would again.

My dad tore across the warehouse parking lot. From outside, the fire alarms and smoke weren't that noticeable. Since it was early on a Saturday morning, all the regular businesses in the warehouse park were closed. The only place open was the indoor playground, and its entrance was all the way at the other end of the lot.

Thankfully, it was also between Fletcher's dad and the parking lot exit. Rath had to slow down the delivery van to steer around some parents and their kids, which gave us the chance to catch up to them.

My dad stomped on the accelerator, ramming the side of the van. It didn't do much to the bigger vehicle, but it got Rafe's attention. He craned his head around to glare at us, then cut the wheel. The delivery van screeched away from us, turning back into the empty section of the parking lot.

"He's heading back toward the warehouse!" I yelled to my dad.

He spun the wheel, our momentum causing the golf cart to tip. As one, we leaned in the opposite direction, until the open-top vehicle was back on all four wheels. My dad mashed the accelerator to the floor, but the cart's electric motor whined in protest.

"This thing only goes, like, twenty-five miles an hour, max," he complained.

"It's probably got a governor," said Brynn. "Keeps people from driving through warehouses at freeway speeds." She scooted to the floor and lifted up the back seat. Underneath it there was open access to the cart's chassis.

"Are you seriously doing that while we're driving?" said my dad.

"You just catch up to our daughter." My stepmom stuck her good foot down into the web of spinning metal parts, and kicked a spinning metal rod until it broke free.

The engine gave a roar. We shot forward as if we'd been kicked by a giant. My dad lost control of the wheel, but quickly got us back on track. We rocketed toward the delivery van at around fifty miles an hour.

"Holy boost power, Batman!" I shouted as my stepmom popped the seat back on. "Where'd you learn how to do that?"

"Benefits of growing up with three brothers," she replied.

Within seconds, our little golf cart had pulled even with the driver's side of the delivery van. Rath scowled and sideswiped us, but my dad kept going straight.

"Now what?" he shouted. "We can't go head-to-head with him—we'll get crushed."

"I'm going over there to get Val," I said. "Just get me close."

"What? Whoa," said Brynn. "You're not a superhero, remember?"

"But I am a big brother. And that a-hole stole my baby sister." I stood on my seat, clutching the top of the windshield for balance. My dad edged closer to the delivery van.

"Be careful!" he called.

And I jumped.

Unfortunately, Fletcher's dad had guessed what I was up to. He cut the van away from us just as I leapt toward them. One of my hands just managed to grab the bar that attached the long sideview mirror on the driver's side of the vehicle. I swung forward, the tips of my sneakers scraping on the speeding concrete beneath me. R-rated, gory visions of my body being crushed beneath delivery van filled my brain, but I gave them a mental drop-kick. I had a sister to save, so I hung on.

"Bravo," said Fletcher's dad sarcastically. "You're a real hero now.

But you know what happens to heroes? They get *killed.*"

WHAM! On the last word, the older man slammed his fist into my fingers. Spikes of pain shot up my arm, but still I hung on. I latched onto the sideview mirror with my other hand, braced my feet against the van, and pulled open the driver's-side door.

WHUMP. Rath took his right foot off the accelerator and kicked me in the gut. I nearly fell, but I just managed to keep hold of the mirror.

I pulled myself into the cab of the car and grabbed the wheel. There was a brief tug-of-war that made the van jerk back and forth over the parking lot. We were now on a collision course with the indoor playground. Seeing me struggle, Val gave a concerned peep from her spot in the passenger seat.

Rath socked me in the gut. My grip on the wheel loosened, and he placed a foot on my chest. "Say bye-bye, big brother."

Then he kicked me out of the van.

I fell backward, nothing but air between me and the concrete below. I pinwheeled my arms, searching for something, anything to grab hold of. I came up empty. Dimly, I knew I probably shouldn't land on my head or spine. I tried to curl my body up, but I only had about three milliseconds of drop time, and I'd already used two of them. I closed my eyes, wincing in preparation for the impact—

But instead I landed on something soft and rubbery. The back seat of the golf cart. Brynn had climbed to the front, and my dad had swooped in as my safety net.

I allowed myself a groan of relief. "Nice catch," I said.

In the delivery van, Val hadn't seen where I landed. She strained against her seat belt, trying to look outside and fussing. "Ra ba?" she asked.

"Ugh, shut up," said Rafe, actually covering her mouth with his hand.

She did not like that. Val jerked her head away, screaming in anger: "RA! BA!" She furrowed her brow. Then for the first time, without any cues or protective instincts to guide her, she chose to use all her powers.

A magnetic bubble enveloped the delivery van. Metal buckled. The windshield shattered. Bands of electricity zapped Rafe's body. The wheels of the heavy vehicle even floated a few inches above the ground for a moment—

And then it crashed back down to the concrete. The van tipped, rolling end over end across the parking lot. It finally landed on its side, skidding toward the big window of the indoor playground.

CRASH! The van hopped the curb and burst through the window. Shards of glass rained down. The back doors of the car burst open, spilling irradiated pill bottles all over the ground. Kids and caregivers inside screamed and scattered. The vehicle came to rest against a large two-story ball pit.

My dad stopped the golf cart outside the building and I ran inside. He followed behind me, my stepmom leaning on his shoulder. Luckily, it looked like no one inside the playground had been hurt. But the real concern was my baby sister.

"Val?" I shouted, quickly picking my way over piles of glass and metal to reach the front of the van. "Valley, are you okay?"

There was a familiar *boing*, and the chubby cutie floated out of the open door of the delivery van. She laughed delightedly upon seeing me, clapping her teeny hands. When she was close enough, she dropped into my arms.

"Raba, Raba, Raba," she burbled excitedly.

I beamed. "That's right, Robbie! I'm your brother, Robbie!" Cuddling her to my chest, I turned to my dad and Brynn. "Did you guys hear that? Val just said her first word, and it was 'Robbie'!"

"Raba!" shouted Val.

"First steps and her first word all on the same day?" My dad smiled proudly. "She really is a Superkid."

Brynn squinched one eye. "Would we call that a word? I say the jury's still out on that one."

"Aw, stop lawyering. You're just jealous." I kissed Val on her itty-bitty noggin.

Clang. A bruised, bloody hand clapped onto the side of the van, straining until it heaved Rath Grossman into view. He had a big purple bruise on his bald head and his nose was mashed to the side. I hoped it would make him ugly for the rest of his life.

Fletcher's dad limped from the wreckage of the delivery van, dragging his right leg behind him. The shin of his cargo pants was torn and bloody below the knee, and his foot was bent at an angle that can only be described as "super-broken."

"This . . . isn't . . . over," he hissed, gritting his teeth through what I could only hope was excruciating pain. "I won't . . . lose . . . to a kid."

"Your ankle looks like a piece of wet spaghetti," I informed him. "And you didn't lose to a kid. You lost to a *baby.*"

"Wrong," he replied, grabbing a pill bottle off the ground and unscrewing the cap. "I don't lose." He shook the yellow pills into his mouth, chewing and swallowing by the dozen.

"Seriously?" asked Brynn wearily. "Just let it go already."

But Rath twitched as the massive amount of Fortis radiation hit his system. His pupils expanded and began to vibrate. "Yesss . . ." he said, standing up straighter. "I see why the guards go crazy for this stuff. That is . . . nice."

Crack! Fletcher's dad put his thumbs to either side of his broken nose and twisted, resetting the bone. Everyone in the indoor playground winced, but Fletcher's father seemed to feel no pain. He walked toward us, the bones of his busted ankle scraping wetly against one another. The sound and sight of it was enough to make most of us look away.

"That is so not right," I said.

"You people, you don't deserve a Superkid," he said as he drew closer. "I'm the only one who can realize her full potential."

"And I'm her father," said my dad. "So my wife and I will decide what's best for her."

He stepped in front of me, but Rath Grossman's hands shot forward in a blur. He grabbed my father by his shirt, tossing him against the side of the delivery van as if he weighed no more than a scarecrow.

Brynn stepped in front of me next, but Rath karate chopped her in the solar plexus. My stepmom doubled over, wheezing. The playground bystanders objected, but none of them came to our aid. After seeing what Fletcher's dad was capable of, I can't say I blamed them.

It was just me versus the Fortis-jacked psychopath now. "You might be able to knock down us regular folks," I said. "But that doesn't hold true with a Super—"

WHAP! Before I could even point my sister at him, Rath Grossman punched Val in the face.

That's right. An adult man filled to the brim with strength-increasing, pain-lessening pills coldcocked a *baby*. Val's head snapped back, then her eyes closed and her body went slack. The whole room recoiled in disgust and shock.

"See that?" said Rath to the appalled crowd. "Three months, he's been living with a superhero, and he still doesn't understand her. Can't use her powers if she's"—he tilted up Val's head, then let it fall back down—"totally unconscious." He smiled nastily. "Everyone has their kryptonite, I guess. Now hand her over."

I started to back away. "She's my family. You're gonna have to kill me to take her."

Rath shrugged. "Okay."

His hand shot out, wrapping around my neck. I shifted Val to one arm, using my free hand to pull at Rafe's fingers, but they were as immovable as iron bars. He squeezed even tighter. Red balloons began to swell and pop before my eyes. The supervillain's triumphant, vibrating eyeballs were only six inches from mine.

"Stupid kid," he whispered. "All you're doing is giving your sister a great origin story."

A roaring sound filled my ears. I assumed it was from all the blood that was being prevented from reaching my brain. But then I saw a blurry beige shape loom large in the corner of my eye.

Fletcher drove the second golf cart directly into his father. Rath went flying into the ball pit. His son hit the brakes, but his speed and the glass-covered floor didn't exactly allow the vehicle to stop on a dime. He crashed into the ball pit's steel support column. The front of the golf cart crumpled, crushing Fletcher's pelvis.

The pain must have been terrible, or maybe it was so terrible that he didn't feel it all, because my former best friend was able to lift his curly orange head and make eye contact with his father. "Whoops," he said through bloodstained teeth. "Guess you shoulda taught me how to drive after all." Then his head fell forward and he passed out.

Rath awkwardly sat up. He was bruised and bloody and for a moment his eyes looked like those of any father concerned for his son. Then they began to vibrate again, and he focused on me. "You did this," he hissed. "You turned him against me."

I massaged my bruised windpipe, trying to speak in something other than a croak. "I think you did that on your own."

"I. Am Going. To kill you," Fletcher's dad said, wading through the ball pit toward me.

Gently, I laid my unconscious sister on the floor. Then I stepped in front of her, weaving and barely able to stay on my feet. The room was still filled with large red balloons. I shook my head to make them pop. Rath leapt from the ball pit, his broken ankle hitting the ground with a wet *crunch*. He started toward me—

But a big hand fell on his shoulder. It belonged to an average-looking dad in shorts and a T-shirt that actually said GOLF! on it. "Hold up, baldy," Average Dad said in a firm voice. "You hit a baby, you gotta deal with me, too."

More adult caregivers of all shapes and sizes began to step forward. "Me too," said a brawny mother in her forties.

"And me," said a bearded, tough-looking biker dad.

"And me," added a bubble-gum-chewing teenage babysitter in a tank top and short shorts.

"And us," echoed two sweater-vested grandpas in unison.

By now at least a dozen adults stood between me and my baby sister. And they looked pissed. Rath barked a laugh. "You breeders think you can frighten me? I'm on Fortis. I'm invincib— Hey! Stop it. Get your hands off me!"

The meteorite may have temporarily given Fletcher's dad the strength of ten men, but ten men were still no match for two dozen angry caregivers. Dads, moms, grandpas, babysitters, and older siblings all converged on Rath Grossman, dragging him back to the ball pit and lashing him so tightly to the wall netting that all he could do was blink.

As much as I would have loved to help, the morning's exertions had finally caught up with me. I sank back down to the floor and lifted Val into my lap. As I gently stroked her chubby little face, I allowed my eyes to close. I had earned five minutes of rest, especially now that I knew there were people other than myself who were willing to protect the world's first superhero.

My head fell to my chest, and for the first time in what felt like years, I fell into a deep, carefree sleep.

So there you have it. The absolutely true, stinky-diapers-and-all origin story of the world's first infant superhero.

Things didn't end there, naturally. Several people at the indoor playground notified 911, as well as the local police, fire department, paramedics, Instagram, Facebook, Snapchat, and every other social media site with a goofy name. An hour later the parking lot was swarming with first responders. The factory fires were put out, the bullet was removed from my stepmom's leg, and all our various bruises, scrapes, and abrasions were bandaged. Val also woke up, recovering from her first punch like a champ.

Only the Grossmans had sustained really serious injuries. When the paramedics arrived, they found the lower portion of Fletcher's spine had been crushed against the front seat support bar. They were unsure if he'd ever walk again. As my former friend was loaded into the back of an ambulance bound for the nearest hospital, he stopped the EMTs and waved me over. Grudgingly, I went to his side.

"I'm sorry," he said, salt water welling in his eyes. "I didn't mean for things to get so messed up. I just wanted my life to be . . . special."

"Everybody wants that, dummy," I told him. "Doesn't mean you can go around using other people like action figures."

He nodded, then grabbed his hip and winced. Looked like his injuries were finally starting to register. Hopefully, the pain would make him take stock of what he and his psycho-dad had done. "I got delivery on a vintage *Green Lantern* issue the other day. Art by Neal Adams himself. Maybe . . . we can swap someday?"

Despite his actions, I couldn't fully hate Fletcher. You don't just forget your best friend in a single evening. I wasn't sure if we'd ever be able to hang out again, and I certainly wasn't going to make it easy for him. "I don't know. But thanks for . . . you know, driving in at the end there. It was"—I searched for a word that was descriptive, but fair—"heroic."

He gave me a sad, bittersweet smile, then the paramedics shut the ambulance doors. As the emergency vehicle pulled away, I looked over the aftermath of our showdown with the Grossmans. Rafe's mercenaries had been rounded up by the police and handcuffed, as had their former boss. Once the Fortis wore off, Fletcher's dad was much easier to manage. Unfortunately, his weakened state didn't prevent him from screaming insults at us as the cops dragged him away.

"That girl's powers, they're only going to get stronger!" he shouted at us. "You really think you're going to be able to handle her by yourselves? You??" His broken ankle banged against the door of the police van. "Ahh! Police brutality, you cretins."

"We'll figure it out," my dad said, putting an arm around me and Brynn. "That's what family does."

Val blew a raspberry at the wannabe supervillain.

"Wave 'bye-bye,'" I said to her, moving her chubby fist up and down in Rafe's direction. "'Cause he's going to *pri-son for-ev-er*."

"I'll get out," said Fletcher's dad confidently. "Rich people don't go to prison in this country. And when I get out, I will come for—

OWWW!" he shouted as the cops shut the door on his busted ankle.

"Thank you," Brynn called to them. The cops gave us a tiny salute.

A boxy, no-nonsense, government-issue Ford Taurus pulled into the warehouse lot. A woman exited the front passenger seat, sporting a bland business suit, oversized sunglasses, and a no-frills haircut I recognized immediately. She didn't pause to take in the scene, but walked straight toward us.

"Agent Burgertime," I said, then caught myself. "Bergerschmidt, sorry. Fletcher really did a number on me."

"In more ways than one, I observe," she replied in a flat, emotionless voice. She turned to the suited federal underling next to her. "Notify Homeland that we have a positive ID on our fugitives."

My family and I looked at one another, worried. "Does that mean . . . you're arresting us?" asked my stepmom, preparing to shift into Lawyer Mode.

Bergerschmidt's face was as impassive as ever. "Don't be silly. But do remove their names from the Most Wanted list," she added to her lackey. "They're safe now."

She took off her sunglasses. The corners of her mouth twitched upward. Her lips pulled back to show some actual teeth. "Are you . . . smiling?" I asked in disbelief.

"I believe that's the customary way to express happiness." Then her face returned to its usual, resting scowl. "Thank God that's over. It hurts my cheeks. I'm pleased to see you four alive and well. You fled before I could explain that your best friend and his father were sociopathic criminals."

"Yeah, we figured that out," my dad said sarcastically. "No thanks to you guys."

"I'm afraid our investigation was classified," the Homeland Security agent replied crisply. "We've been surveilling the Grossmans for nearly two years, and we couldn't afford to let them know we were onto them. Their theft of the meteorite last week gave us the final confirmation we needed to arrest him."

"Then why did you come to *our* house at five in the morning and shoot off live ammunition?" Brynn asked in disbelief.

"Had your son not booby-trapped the entrances, we would have never drawn our weapons. But enough catching up." Bergerschmidt clapped her hands. "We've got a lot to do before you can meet the others."

The last word thudded on my eardrums like a nuclear bomb. "Other . . . whats?" I asked cautiously.

Bergerschmidt looked at me, the corners of her mouth once more twitching upward slightly. "The other superkids, of course."

My parents and I looked at one another. I already had a big dumb grin on my face, but they were more anxious. "But . . . I thought . . . Rath said . . ." my dad stammered.

"Rath Grossman knew even less than his son about how many people were exposed to Fortis. Thankfully, we sequestered the other kids before the Grossmans knew they existed."

"So how many of them are out there?" I asked, trying to contain my excitement.

"Including Val? Three. But we expect to find more before the year is out. We've already got a great training facility—top secret location, plenty of safety features, and the best kinder care experts in the nation. The world has changed, and now we're all toddling to catch up. But don't worry—we'll get there."

The Homeland agent ruffled my baby sister's hair like a robot patting a dog. Then she stood upright, facing each one of us in turn. "So what do you say? Care to join the country's most exclusive day care?"

I turned to my parents, seeing they were still dazed by what Bergerschmidt had said. I reminded myself that less than a month had passed since they'd learned their infant daughter had superpowers. I could see they needed a little more processing time. It was up to me to handle this, and I knew just what to say.

I cleared my throat, folded my arms, and gave the agent my best lawyerly stare. "That depends. What sort of terms are you offering?"

ACKNOWLEDGMENTS

I first had the idea for *Superkid* back in 2014. In the seven years since then, many people helped shape the story into the book you're holding today. Elizabeth Arredondo read an early version and suggested I change the main character from a stay-at-home dad to an older sibling. She was correct. Thank you, Liz.

John Fletcher loaned me his name, his prodigious comic book knowledge, and his companionship at nearly every Marvel movie. (He would also like me to tell you that he looks nothing like the Fletcher of this book.) Nora McFarland gave me some helpful notes about changing Robbie's background, even if she was talking about a different book. I'm grateful to them both.

In 2015, I wrote and co-directed a short film called *Super Kids: Epic Showdown* for YouTube. Working on the project helped me visualize some of the ideas that I was kicking around for this novel. Thank you Daniel Hashimoto and the folks at 1st Avenue Machine for asking me to be a part of it.

Kaitlin Severini provided excellent copyediting and helped me double-check the geography of San Francisco. Thank you, Kaitlin. Any errors or fabrications are my fault, mostly because they worked better for the story.

Thanks to Juliane Crump for designing the book cover and interior illustrations. She endured my queries about when it would be done with grace and patience.

This novel owes a great debt to the nearly ninety years of superhero storytelling that have come before me. Thank you to all the artists, writers, and filmmakers who brought those stories to life and provided me with so much inspiration.

Finally, I'm grateful to my wife and two sons for giving me so much time to write books. Time is the greatest gift of all, and I appreciate it on a daily basis.

Matt Harry, January 2021

CPSIA information can be obtained
at www.ICGtesting.com
Printed in the USA
BVHW030006010621
608485BV00020B/205